To Cousin Mic.
from. Cousin Hilda.

A little peek into
my Heart.

Sep 3/2009

Hilda Nightingale

I Talk To Dragonflys

by

Hilda Nightingale

authorHOUSE®

AuthorHouse™
1663 Liberty Drive, Suite 200
Bloomington, IN 47403
www.authorhouse.com
Phone: 1-800-839-8640

First published by AuthorHouse 12/5/2008

ISBN: 978-1-4343-7997-9 (sc)
ISBN: 978-1-4343-7996-2 (hc)

Printed in the United States of America
Bloomington, Indiana

This book is printed on acid-free paper.

ACKNOWLEDGEMENT

To my daughter Brenda and granddaughter Tamara.
Without their help this book would have remained
Just thoughts.

DEDICATION

This book is for my children

BRENDA
ROBERT
DEBORAH
COLLEEN

CONTENTS

x

THIS IS A MEMORY

Yesterday, gone, used up
A page in a diary, a thought

A regret, a tear,
All the days and hopes of a year

Pushed behind today, and forgotten
Until we need a moment to remember
A nice thing that happened last September

And then all the hours flood back
To hurt, make us laugh, smile
And to warm us for awhile

THE DRAGONFLY

Sometimes we are privileged to experience the majesty and mysteries of
nature
One autumn afternoon. While enjoying the last warm rays of the setting
sun, I noticed a fluttering in the corner of my rose trellis.
Looking closer I saw a dragonfly caught in a spider web. I saw it struggle
and felt the terror it must be feeling, knowing what would happen.
I put my hand under its body and lifted it from the web, and with a
pine needle cleared the web off the back legs.
It made no attempt to fly away until the sticky web was gone. I
marveled at the beautiful black Body and silver wings.
It then flew into the sky like a plane from a landing field and did loop-
de-loops and soared in every direction.
It finally returned and landed on my hand again, it raised and lowered
its wings several times before flying into the sky and disappearing
Leaving me with such a feeling of awe, and a beautiful memory to last
me the rest of my life.

MIRROR OF TIME

Tears we shed for what our lifetime might have been
As heartaches plague our every day
And though we try to hold to hope
We lose our dreams along the way
We cannot fool our hearts, and so
The dreams replaced by what is here
And in the mirror of our time
We see a stranger standing there
We compensate with change of thought
It`s made us cautious and aware
The path we saw ahead in youth
Now will not take us anywhere
There is the bold that won't be led
But I will take the quiet path
That takes no courage, straight ahead
For I am tired out, and old
I've lost the will to change my pace
And it is mirrored hundred fold
In every old and wrinkled face
In eyes that held a far off dream
Now faded, hardly recognized
That no amount of thought will ever ream
And gone before we realize
I do not look from left to right
For if I do, I may see youth
Holding forth a future day
All golden bright with shining time
And fat with dreams, and polished hope
And throw my caution right away
And think that I can start again
And wear the sunlight in my eyes
And listen not to somber thoughts
And throw away those whispered lies
Forget these weary bones, and dance
And storm the castle walls again
Pick up the gauntlet and the lance
But it was just a moment's trick
A change of thought, or something said
For I stay on the quiet path
That takes no courage, straight ahead

NEED

I hope someone will say of me
I knew her well, and liked her style
And how I miss her now she's gone
I wish we'd meet and talk awhile

She made me feel a worthwhile friend
As though I counted in her day
I feel emptiness inside
Now that she has gone away

Oh how we need to feel our worth
To fill a need in someone's heart
For loneliness can bruise the soul
And absence makes the teardrops start

I hope that thinking of me now
Sends special smiles, right to your heart
And knowledge that I'm always near
Even though were miles apart

THIS PROMISE LAND

If man should leave this earth I know
No one would mourn to see him go
The world would be a better place
And would not miss the human race

The trees would grow the brooks would run
And nature's works would still be done
And earth again would be all green
And not a man made thing is seen

And time would pass, with night and day
I know if nature had her way
That soon the very act of man
Would not be seen upon this land

And everything would balance out
Left all alone, there is no doubt
That time and nature hand in hand
Would set to right this Promise Land

IT`S UP TO YOU

Against the distant sunset far
Behind the castle wall

With reaching fingers gold and red
I hear the twilight call

As she wraps her misty mantle
Round another dying day

She claim's the unused hours
And takes them far away

And what she takes, she won't return
But starts you out anew

So what you use tomorrow for
Is up to you

MYSELF

I long ago have lost myself
In what I think that I should be
In a forest of actions I have learned
In what my days have made of me

It is too late to ever change
For I have lost me long ago
So I must urge this stranger on
To keep up with the human flow

Sometimes I search this distant heart
When things are still, and I am near
I see a shadow quiet, gray
A whispered voice I can't quite hear

And though I want this distant self
It's always, as I fear
I reach to touch my shadow
But I just disappear

OVER THE HILL

Along the lane and over the hill
There's a little cottage that stands there still

A place in my dreams, I used to reside
With a crystal brook running beside

And a giant oak with an old rope swing
With sprawling arms where the robins sing
Someday I'll go back where my calling heart
Beckons me home, where I had my start
With the warmth of feelings I remember still
Along the lane and over the hill

THE OLD MANS GRAVE

They laid the old man cold and deep
Without a thought or care
Nobody came to see him off
No one from anywhere

He was not thought in any mind
No tear in any eye
Nor missed in any single heart
Nor marked where he would lie

The years slipped by, I chanced to pass
That long forgotten spot
The old mans grave, was covered with
Wild blue forget-me-nots

MY REVERIE

I close my eyes; accept the gentle gift of sleep
That ends the weary day
I drift and dream of wondrous things
And places far away

Then I am all I wish to be
In any place I deem
No trouble touches this my heart
When I lie down and dream

I do not smell the flowers
But join them in their bed
And speak to birds up in the sky
Though not a word is said

And when the sun of morn invades my sleep
And seeks my reverie to take
I hold this elusive slumber, if I can
For I don't want to wake

REACH OUT

Today there is no sadness in my heart
Today the sun will warm my ageing bones
And happiness is just within my reach
It shades me with its textures and it's tones

Yesterday fast fades from memories view
My sorrows now are dulled like pewter gray
My change of heart is slow I eke it out
As if I cannot let them get away

And still I reach and though I hesitate
It's only that I've been through this before
If I except whole heart and mind
What will tomorrow have for me in store?

But I must take this chance and reach
And grasp at life, if only for awhile
And savor each experience in time
Each day, and even dare to smile

GROWING OUT

Take my hand and lead me on
Down the highway of my years
There may be rocks of sorrow
Pitfalls of shedded tears

And I may fall or stumble
And may not see the signs
Because of looking backwards
At the memories in my mind

For we all take warmth and comfort
From the things we felt before
And are loath to search for new things
And too weak to close the door

And so we never grow and learn
For the changes that we make
Will feed our days
And lead us in directions that we take

Sometimes we make decisions
That will blind us and allure
And our ego takes a bruising
That's the way that we mature

But if we stay still, stagnant
And do only what we know
It's certain that we stay the same
And never ever grow

WHEN SHADOWS FALL

When shadows fall across the grass
I do not dream about the dawn
But watch the midnight sky alight
With all the stars that night will spawn

And there are those that feel like me
Who see the wonder see my sky
And do not take a ready word
But seem like me, to question why

For in this shadowed other world
That hides the answers from our sight
And lends a promise with the moon
And paints the way with silver light

And only those that pass the stars
Can hope in part to glimpse a sign
The weave and texture of the years
The tapestry of life's design

COUNTING BLESSINGS

Every day tasks they take time, but with pride
I wash up the dishes and put them aside
With bread in the oven, and clothes on the line
I clean up the floor, just look at the time
With all of the work, the days slipping by
And finally it's ended, I sit with a sigh
I'm tired and weary, but snug up above
In clean beds lay sleeping the ones that I love
And a feeling comes stealing as I take a rest
And a thought fills my heart of how much I am blessed

JOURNEY IN THOUGHT

Sometimes my mind will soar in flight
Just like a bird on wing
And enter some forgotten realm
Remember some forgotten thing
And nest it in mind's vision
To savor it once more
Some tidbit back from long ago
From our subconscious store
And eye will picture distant things
Thoughts journey far and wide
To bring to light our treasures deep
With only memory to guide

THE OLD MAN'S STORY

I listened to the old man
And the story that he told
He said you don't know sadness
Until you've grown old
Accepting all life's goodness
But we in youth forget
We all take life for granted
Till we look back in regret
Yes we take all life will offer
And we never stop to think
That all we have and hold so dear
Can vanish in a wink
I listened to the old man
Looked in his faded eyes
And saw the far off wisdom
And knew they were not lies
But would I heed his warning
Or just go my merry way
And repeat regrets and warnings
To another youth someday
Perhaps some of his wisdom
Will linger in my ear
Perhaps I'll see those faded eyes
And all he had to bear
I remember sometimes
The story that he told
There seemed to be so many years
Before I grew that old
Yes I remember vaguely
A haunting memory
In distant past a story
An old man told to me

COURAGE

What happened to the courage of my youth?
The zeal I felt at facing each new dawn
The future that had held such worthwhile plans
That seemed the reason that I had been born

What turn in life upon the road ahead I made
That seemed to lead my dreams astray
I did not know I drifted from the path
Just where and how and when I lost my way

And only with the years of looking back
And searching all my days for past mistakes
I find neglect and disregard of time
And many faults that all we mortals make

Opportunities that never come again
And if were seen were never acted on
Such apathy snuffed out the youthful dreams
And at long last there is not even one

But should we really shoulder all the blame
Intentions are the biggest part of dreams
Tomorrow seen in such a rosy glow
They do not light our way except they gleam

So unattended thus my dreams did die
I fed them not with hope or kept them new
But left them there to keep themselves
They faded and no longer came to view

WHEN TWILIGHT COMES

When twilight comes I hold my own
For then I let my feelings roam
As shadows fill the corner stair
And see the phantoms waiting there
They do not always look the same
Each night they have a different name

And as the twilight's wearing thin
I let my fancy reel and spin
I sail, I dance, I even sing
I feel I could do anything
My clothing then is spun of gold
And I am free and I am bold

Sometimes I am a lovely rose
Sometimes I am a twinkle toes
Never tired never sad
My heart is full of joy and glad
With jelly tarts and bubble punch
For breakfast, supper even lunch

No one to censor or to say
Save some to eat another day
When twilight fades and travels far
And nighttime comes with Silver Star
The phantoms creep away, away
And even daylight cannot stay

The blackness steals all waking thought
And phantoms rest, as well they ought
Until another twilight starts
With bubble punch and jelly tarts

DREAMING

I walked through memories garden
Through trees and flowers there
And found a child who had been chained
To worldly woe and care

I saw a happy smiling face
Reflected in a stream
And golden hair now faded gray
Alive with sunlight sheen

I ran along the yellow grass
And talked to birds on wing
And floated high among the clouds
And heard my own heart sing

If this be dreaming, let me dream
Till bluebells softly chime
I have not lost myself at all
I've been here all the time

TIME TRAVEL

I remember yesterday
When I did not feel so old
And my thoughts were of the future
And the winters weren't so cold
And anything was possible
And I loved with all my heart
And I clung to life and felt the earth
Each day a brand new start
And hope would glow in every morn
And days were precious, rare
Each minute new adventure
With just my being there
And I traveled far within my mind
To futures golden bright
Until I could not see at all
So blinded by it's light
And had I stayed within my mind
And not emerged from thought
I would have stayed sublimely vague
My heart would not be caught
Upon the now and evermore in cold realities
I would have stayed with yesterday
And lofty memories

LITTLE BITS OF HEAVEN

Little bits of heaven drop to earth
From time to time
They bloom the rose and leaf the tree
And make the bluebells chime
Like tiny chips of stars
They brighten up the days
And smooth the rocky roads
Along the yearly ways
They sparkle on the flowers
They twinkle on the grass
And look like diamonds to the eye
As weary strangers pass
Little bits of heaven drop to earth
From time to time
And soothe the soul and rest the heart
And some are yours and mine

THE CIRCLE

I remember you at two
I helped you then each day you grew
Learning, and though very small
I measured you against the wall
I remember you at five
So full of life and so alive
I saw your independence grow
You helped yourself and let me know
I remember you at ten
Your manliness, yes even then
The picture of the years to come
The adding up the total sum
And now I see you fully grown
And you can manage all alone
And I am sad but justly proud
And help sometimes when I'm allowed
The years have gone, I know not where
The childhood days soon disappear
And now my son you are a man
And you may give a helping hand
To one who lives life as a child
And lets you help, once in a while

THE RACE

I know that you are close
In physical form, but still
I cannot feel your loving warmth
And though I try I never will
Why do I strive, and yearn to touch
And practice my deceit
We seem to be a world apart
And only in my mind is union sweet
But what is left of life
If I were suddenly to call a halt
And know my dreams for what they are
And loose love's battle, by default
Then life to me would be a race
That I have run without a prize
The consequences I will face
Are pain and torment in disguise
For love is beauty face and form
And does not show her sister strife
And we poor mortals court them both
All our life

THE WEAVERS

We weave our minutes into days
We weave them down our yearly ways
Soft feathers of time of seconds bright
But we must weave them strong and right
To hold for us in time ahead
All the things we've thought and said
And like the egg within the nest
We lay each memory to rest
In time to finally break apart
To fly and warm our days, our heart
And some will go and not return
And some will make us weep and yearn
And some will fly just out of reach
And some have lessons they will teach
That even thoughts are not our own
We travelers do not age alone
But ever twining down the years
Our dreams and loves, our hates and fears
Seen mirrored in another's eye
The puzzled look. the question why
So if we lend a helping hand
And join the ever growing band
Of wisdom seekers, gaining heart
In knowledge that we are a part
Of all the dreamers, condescend
To weave our dreams unto the end

MY MOTHER

Who worked from early morning light?
And after were in bed at night
And taught us all to do the right
My mother

Who gave herself with lasting zeal?
With not too much could make a meal
And showed us how to love and feel
My mother

Who told us there was someone there
To help us through our hurt and fear
To take our hand and really care
My mother

Who left us with the knowledge of
A God with everlasting love
That we would meet again above
My mother

THE BLUE LACE DRESS

Lizzy was lonely, and all alone
She didn't have a telephone
She didn't even know how to play
So she stayed in her room all the day
Lizzy was lonely ,yes indeed
She had no books so she could not read

She had no pet, dog or cat
She had no coat, she had no hat
Lizzy was lonely and she didn't know
That down in a house in the valley below
There lived a lady, sad and poor
All alone when she closed the door

She had one wish when she prayed each night
For a little girl that would fit her right
Every time she went to town
She carried a little blue lace gown
Just in case she happened to see
A little girl with a please take me

The little old lady looked up high
But all she could see were trees and sky
She did not know that waiting there
Was one little girl that would really care
This little girl with the freckled face
Who would love to have a pale blue lace

And someone to care and someone to love
But she was high in the hills above
then one night came a falling star
The valley folk saw it and followed it far
It led them up the great tall hill
And some of them are up there still

The little old lady went along
Carried the lace and humming a song
When the little girl saw the pale blue lace
Her eyes grew large in her freckled face
Are you alone the lady said
As she slipped the blue dress over her head

It wasn't loose, it wasn't tight
In fact the dress just fit her right
And the old lady hugged her and realized
That this little girl was just the right size
I'm glad I found out where you are
I'm really glad I followed the star

If I hadn't I'm sorry to say
I wouldn't have met you here today
And all the village was happy to see
She was not alone when she took her key
And unlocked the door to her tiny place
By her side was a girl in a pale blue lace

COCOON

Castles of smoke fill my mind
Oh how I guard the vision of my dreams
And though the real days always are around
The dream is when I live, or so it seems
I cling to times that seem so very real
See distant things, they say that are not true
Old ways warm my heart and so
I loathe to turn to anything that's new
But just beyond the fringes of my mind
Lurk shadows that I try to keep at bay
Unwanted guests I will not wine and dine
Even though they will not go away
I know how fragile are the walls of dreams
No bulwark strong against the storms of life
Held only by the dreamers faithful thoughts
And smashed apart by doubting them and strife
A dreamer's path is harder than the rest
A dreamer must be very brave and strong
They find the dreaming time a soft cocoon
And waking times stretch wearily and long
And though we die in dreaming, we must dream
For each of us are what were meant to be
We may leave still dreaming, and believe
We enter into visions that we see

OLD SAD HOUSES

Old houses make me sad
Full of dead dreams
Their glass eyes staring
An invitation, or so it seems

But I'm afraid to enter
Emotions are too strong for me
I cannot stay there undisturbed
I absorb each thing I see

Old paper yellow and torn
Faded spots where pictures hung
Well-worn stairs gray with dust
Chips and scars on every rung

And walls that ring with memories
If you are quiet you can hear
Voices of the long long past
Laughter crying lingers near

But I must go
My heart can hold no more
I leave the aching yesteryears
By just the closing of the door

THESE HANDS

These hands I am ashamed to see
That rest all wrinkled on my knee
There hands not pale like lady fair
And there not even wash and wear
They never donned a rubber glove
They're not the hands that's held in love
These hands have opened many doors
These hands have scrubbed a million floors
They have stroked a weary fevered head
And tucked the children into bed
And they have prayed and wiped a tear
These hands have held a baby near
These hands are here for all to see
They tell the world that I am me
Each spot and wrinkle, broken nail
Will tell who looks, my life long tale
They do the best each day I live
These hands have reached to all to give
And if you take a second look
You read these hands just like a book

DON`T MAKE LOVE WITH STRANGERS

No words of love were spoken
As he held her close and tight
No words of love were spoken
As they made love that night

And in the early morning
Just at the break of dawn
No words of love were spoken
He was gone

And she felt sad and empty
For she will not forget
He held her close and held her tight
And took her precious gift

Wherever you are lover
Perhaps with someone new
Don't speak of love to strangers
But please remember who

Gave you her love forever
As you held her close and tight
Though no words of love were spoken
Through that night

MY COTTAGE

Along a little country road
Not paved but gravel still
A tiny little cottage stands
All nestled in the hill
A serene and restful picture
With nothing else about
Except a soft gray plume of smoke
Atop the chimney spout
Oh what a restful picture
And finally to stay
Reality of a memory
I carried while away
There must be a distant treasure
To dwell a dream upon
Some place to please the heart and soul
When everything is done
More real it is by far
Than memories faded will
My cottage small inviting me
All nestled in the hill

JOYFUL HEARTS

The mirror tells me I am old
But had it not been there
I would have thought myself to be
Still oh so young and fair
I would have entered into life
With joyous stride and spring
And romped with all of nature
And caught the golden ring
Mirrors are so truthful
They show us as we are
They let us see the steps ahead
The old age door ajar
But joyful hearts say that we are young
So dance along your way
Tomorrow we will all be old
But not today

LOVES MOMENT

This will be a short love
Then I'll have to go
I just remembered there is
Some other girl I know
A walk out in the moonlight
Perhaps a kiss or two
This will be a short love
Then my friend were through
Well maybe a long talk
A little holding hands
You know when we talk love
It leads to golden bands
Now my sweet it's over
I'm leaving in the morn
I'll take your memory with me
So don't look so forlorn

OUR PAY

If every year is measured by the treasures that we keep
And every day is thought as good by conquests that we reap
And we only see the value in what we have at hand
And we work each day just for the coin that's always in demand
Then we lose sight of living and our day is spent in vain
And we use our time in gathering that's all we ever gain
We don't broaden our horizons or enlarge our scope to see
We remain so small and narrow and that's all we'll ever be
For in our daily living if we don't take time to grow
How will we learn about the world how will we ever know?
That butterfly's can rest with ease upon a daisy head
We'll never see a mother bird, or how her babies fed
Or watch a maple shed her leaves all crimson in the fall
And see the sunset in the west then hear a night bird call
Or feel the need of many as we journey through our days
For It's only when we listen that we learn to mend our ways
And lend a hand to someone and try to fill a need
And overcome our selfishness thoughtlessness and greed
For there's merit in a lifetime spent in giving, and you'll find
That for every good deed that we do, life pays us back in kind

THE MISSING MAN

If you ever chance to meet
A faceless man on silent feet
With no opinion voice or call
For life will move him not at all
Then you have met a man today
Who sees no black or white just gray
Who feels no empathy or tear
From anything that he might hear
The summer breeze accepted and
He does not see the flowers stand
He sees no view from yonder hill
Nor hears the wren or whippoorwill
And people, shadows passing by
He greets no one or questions why
The years of silence slip away
He kept all living life at bay
They said a prayer and buried deep
And though they noticed under feet
A single flower growing tall
They did not miss the man at all

IT`S NOT TOO LATE

When all your years are run lad
And all your dreams are dead
And you think without your heart lad
And only with your head
And your days run in together
And your years pass from your view
And life's sounds merge together
And your friends are less than few
Then you have not planted wisely
For the seeds that you have sown
Should now pour forth their bounty
From the years that they have grown
Had you planted deeds of kindness
In your lifelong garden made
You could have reaped the harvest
Used the tree of life for shade
The rose of hope and friendship
Each day without alarm
It would have aided you in living
And protected you from harm
But still there is some time lad
If you don't just sit and wait
For if there's just one spark of life
It's not too late

HIDING

The darkness of the night suits me just fine
I cannot see the man made scars
My vision is curtailed, the distant soft
And reaches only to the distant stars
I seek not morning, that cold dim dawn
That puts me in my place
And takes the velvet warmth of night, and gives
A new day reality that I must face
I wait, until again I may embrace the star filled night
The quiet softness, and I am more or less
Content, and all is right
Time marches on and goes, I know not where
And I see only evening nigh
And as the twilight deepens
I raise my head again unto the sky

I HAD A DREAM

I had a dream that I was small
I was warm and loved and all
The hurting times had never been
And all the world was bright and clean
Across the years from yesterday
A tiny child can lay away
The broken dreams and every plan
That takes the hope from every man
If I could capture child likeness
And lay the jaded old to rest
Then I could spend each precious day
Seeing beauty on its way
Is life then just a state of mind
The road we tread our hearts should find
A way to dream, as we were small
We wouldn't feel the years at all
Then life is beauty it would seem
And pain and worries just a dream

THE OLD TREE AND MEMORY

I saw a tree all gnarled and bent
And fruitless, black and lean
But she can see it as it was
All fresh and young and leafy green
And just behind a shell of home
That was so full of love each day
With many lives and battles fought
Before each went their separate ways
The roses growing on the vine
That filled the summer night with scent
She smells it yet within her mind
This weary woman old and bent
Who watched this dream to its defeat
But sees the beauty just as long
As pictured in her vision sweet
She hears the voices loud and strong
To stay the end but then no more
The earth will claim the centuries past
The sweet pink roses round the door
And there will be no one to say
But just the gnarled tree bent and lean
That there had been the sounds of love
It's just as if they had not been

DEAR DAUGHTER

It seems a sin your never
Going to wear this pretty dress
But wear your blue jeans everywhere to look just like the rest
It's true you look all scrubbed and clean
Your never shy or coy
But dear sometimes I really can not tell you from a boy
Your feet have never felt a heel
You're always in a flat
Your hair tied in a ponytail
Has never seen a hat
Your nose is scrubbed and shiny
Your lips a natural pink
There is not many people that
Can tell you how to think
You are yourself and I am glad
To live in truth and light
We can't improve perfection
On what God has made so right

DUST

Dust and I are not good friends
And if you visit me
You'll come to learn that dust and I
Just never will agree
I shake the dust cloth left and right
And move the bric-a-brac
And everything is shiny
But in minutes dust is back
Sometimes I just ignore it
When I see it lying there
Soft gray fuzz that clings to all
On table and on chair
I pull the blinds so I can't see
This soft gray down ignoring me
It changes my identity
I feel I never will be free
It has the upper hand you see
And if I stand too long maybe
It will even cover me

SEARCHING FOR MEMORIES

A little strip of garden
Maybe a tree or two
The sound of waves upon the shore
A pretty mountain view
But all of these together are very hard to find
Except when I search memories in my mind

A walk upon the wooded lane
The smell of new mown hay
The sunrise in the early morn
The start of each new day
But all of these together are very hard to find
Except when I search memories in my mind

The thought of friends
That I hold dear
The talks we had
The things we share
All of these together are very hard to find
Except when I search memories in my mind

GHOSTLY POET

The days my thoughts will not be still
But taunt my mind and tease my hand
Word pictures I must put to pen
Of things I do not understand
Where come the pictures that I see
In forms I feel I must translate
With flowing lines that fill my page
Those thoughts and words that cannot wait
And all is lost to worldly drill
I'm occupied with forming prose
My hand will race across the page
From whence it comes, nobody knows
And even though I ponder on
By night and day I wonder still
That what I take as lucky gift
Is really by some angel's will
Or ghostly poet who still roams
Invades my dreams and hears me yearn
Gives up his gift to such as me
For I will quote him in return
And I may never ever know
But take this gift and never care
As long as I can write my thoughts
And scatter poems everywhere

MY STORY

I came for a visit
And stayed for awhile
I cried me a tear
And smiled me a smile
I played me a day
And courted a year
And made me some friends
And counted some dear
I met a true love
I loved for a while
I made us a home
I birthed me a child
I started out young
But now I am old
I'm leaving for home
My story told

A LITTLE FAIRY

There's a fairy in my garden
I'm happy that she's there
And I can see her every move
While sitting in my chair

She's bathing in a dewdrop
And drying with a rose
She leaves a lovely perfume
Every where she goes

Some days when I go looking
She's sitting in my tree
Or riding on a humming bird
Or talking to a bee

I do not interrupt her
For I fear she may be cross
And leave my garden, go away
And that would be my loss

A STEP AWAY

There is a world not far away
That keeps you happy everyday
Where thought is of a special kind
A road of sunlight in your mind

You wander in a happy state
And do not leave to chance to fate
A minute or a dream but hold
Till all your days have turned to gold

Do not think back or look to see
Your time as it was wont to be
For would you change the robins song
A green tree growing tall and strong

The evening sky of deepest blue
The silent joy when day is through
For here you may elude the fray
This world is just a step away

ALWAYS

I see a road where flowers grow
And trees stand tall all in a row
With lots of sky just peeping through
The cotton clouds all white and new
There is no change It's always been
This stationary changeless scene
And it will always stay the same
Encompassed in a picture frame

THE SWEETNESS OF LOVE

There was a time when love was new
And days ahead were treasures rare
With minutes full of feelings fine
We lived them then, and held them near
And like the dew upon the rose
We saw our love so crystal clear
We'd need no touch; we'd need no words
Love bloomed by just our being there
But then the winters of neglect
Would touch the dew upon the rose
The crystal drop would disappear
And would come back to only those
Who cried aloud, an anguished cry
Who reached for love through fear and pain
To only those the crystal drop
Would set upon the rose again
Now armed with memory of the past
Love would be cherished, and held dear
To keep the sweetness of the rose
And see the dewdrop resting there

BLACK DAWN

Each breath I take, each step I tread
Is like a dream of being led
I scorn the moon and mock the sun
And at the closing day I've run
So weary from the hours waste
Past minutes with it's misery laced
I see the future practicing
Each minute happiness will bring
And know with black of night
That once again I've lost the fight
Tomorrow fills my mind with fear
Each second brings tomorrow near
Expectations say again
I'll move and act each hour feign
Until the void is filled with lies
And once again I close my eyes
But now alas in gentle sleep
Nowhere in life I find relief
But just to dream of being led
Each breath I take, each step I tread

TRUE LOVE

The depth of love is measured
In the willingness to give
In all we do, in all we say
In every way we live
There is no pause no turning back
When love is deep and true
And every year, it is the same
It's always shiny new
And trough the tragedies of life
True love will hold you fast
You share the tears, you share the pain
And still true love will last
And when that love is taken
And every tear is cried
You face each day without that love
With emptiness inside
Then turn your face to heaven
And pray to one who'll care
And see His love so beautiful
All shining, waiting there

WHAT AM I

Happiness sits just outside my vision
In shadows like tomorrow
I cannot call the new day forth
It does not fit my sorrow

As if they both have their place
And shapes and shades of color
Laced and woven in my days
White hot, to faded gray, and duller

Until the new times come
And I may wear
The elusive coat of happy days
That lingers like a phantom near

But I am armed with memories
And know those days are only lent
For tomorrow takes this joy away
And brings me discontent

MISSED

The other side of the dust cloth
The other end of the broom
I dream about a lot of things
As I move across the room

As I lift and place each article
And rearrange the dust
I think about the little ones
And remember how I fussed

All that wasted energy
And every wasted day
I could have held, I could have rocked
But now there gone away

There are no toys upon the floor
The carpet's clean and neat
There is no jam around the door
From things that they would eat

But most of all its quiet
No crying, laugh or call
The interplay of family
I miss the most of all

IN MY GARDEN

In my garden there are flowers
And I know them all by name
But when I talk they do not speak
And I think that is a shame

I am sure that they have secrets
And such stories they could tell
For I know all their history
And all their faces well

As we spend our time together
I feel a sudden sad despair
That we cannot share our feelings
For I'm sure they know I care

But they bloom and fill my garden
With their beauty everyday
And leave a promise for tomorrow
When they fade and go away

WHAT THE EYE DOES NOT SEE

I don't want to sit and do nothing
Because I'm old and gray
I don't want to miss a moment
I don't want to waste a day
Why, I could be planting a flower
Inviting a friend to tea
I don't want to sit and do nothing
Because that just isn't me

My arms can still hold a baby
My lips sing a lullaby
My heart still savors a sunset
My eyes a butterfly
The feel of the earth in my fingers
The feel of a wooly lamb
I have to be giving and helpful
Because that's how I am

I still like to walk by the seaside
To sit by the tide on a log
Or at home by a crackling fire
The companionship of a dog
So maybe my hair has turned silver
My steps are a little bit slow
But if my thoughts stay ever young
My vim and my vigor won't go

I'll face with joy each tomorrow
I'll live every second each day
Ignoring the fact of my aching back
And even ignoring the gray

TILL WE ARE FREE

Within myself from hidden depths
Comes pain and thoughts of life
Bewildering with haunted dreams
And laced with strife

And mixed therein the feel of hope
As searching in past days
A glimmer now of what had been
Not bright in shades of gray

And with the searching feeling starts
And tears and change of mind
As minutes alter attitudes
And leave the grays behind

And I will trust again because
I cannot live with doubt
For in the distant past I see
What life is all about

And I have once again endured
The trial days of pain
And pushed them far back in my mind
But they will come again

As life repeats its messages
And those with wisdom see
That there is nothing else to have
Till we are free

MY BED

I will stay in bed and dream
I won't attend the fray
No hurt or anguish touches me
If I stay here all day

And soon the night will shed its vale
And softer sights and sounds
And I am comforted with love
I can feel it all around

And I may stay forever
It's tempting just to know
The outside world is over there
A place I will not go

But if I don't know pain and fear
I may not recognize
The opposite is truth and bliss
And here within it lies

The living that we do each day
And we become aware
The give and take that rude exchange
Is how we get our share

REFLECTIONS

Shadows from the past fall across my mind
And I am caught upon a snag a thought a place a time
And I relive a segment of a past experience
And pictures flash and thus emerge across my memory dance

But they have changed I see them now as times I must embrace
The years have mellowed bygone times they've lost their bitter trace
And they have taught me how to feel I use them every day
The memories of the long ago these sentinels in play

What would I be if not the past had lent the guiding hand
To shape and mold the inner me to help me understand
To me I am with minutes tread like building blocks at play
Each word and deed each thing I saw molded me each day

And I can be nobody else no matter how I try
I am the me my life has made until the day I die

THE LITTLE BOY

Oh how he ran to play and fell
And tearfully came home to tell
And mother searched her heart to say
What they are teaching moms today

The books the thoughts are all a muddle
When all she wants to do is cuddle
But would it harm him in some way
Those loving words she'd like to say

Would it make him less when he is grown?
Or weaker when he stands alone
Perhaps the tenderness mom's feel
Would help the hurt and make it heal

Perhaps the words a baby hears
Could make him tender in his years
When he is tall and faces out
To figure what it's all about

A tender heart can't make us weak
A memory from a time so sweet
But answers from the past to stay
The questions of a grown up day

THE CABIN

Do you hear the north wind mother?
Is the larder stocked up good?
Have you made the jam and smoked the ham
I've chopped ten cords of wood

Do you feel the chill wind mother?
Now nights are long and black
Light the old wood stove mother
And I'll bring another stack

Do you hear that moaning mother?
Pull your shawl around you tight
Get your chair and pull it near
For we won't sleep tonight

In the spring the silent cabin
A mute testimony stood
The chimney dark the woodshed stark
In the quiet of the wood

GHOSTLY GUARD

I saw him tread his weary way
His rifle shouldered high
I watched the tears run down his cheeks
I heard his plaintive cry

His eyes held visions not for me
No muse to fill my mind
His lips would utter not a word
His face with sadness lined

His stance erect and purposeful
He moved with soundless tread
Among the crosses row on row
That held the long lost dead

No grasses had his purpose bent
His tour of duty through
Presented arms and bowed his head
And faded from my view

ONE REFRAIN

I stood in the shadows and watched every day
The minutes the hours the years tick away
And the plans in my heart and my mind as a child
Were either discarded or finally filed

The shadows grew longer and darker and I
Knew nobody saw or heard my faint cry
The child in me waited for patience was learned
And destiny laughed to see I still yearned

Did the years leave no hope for the years left to come?
Can you fill your time with a heart that is numb?
As I look back to see the child waiting there
I only see shadows that's all that appear

So lost in the past that I cannot recall
The dreams of a child that don't count at all
Had I known that the future was so predefined
The road that I thought straight would so twist and wind
Would I still have ventured sing just one refrain?
And draw on the courage to try it again

THEN AND NOW

I remember days of yore
When I was young and insecure
When thoughts of love would give a rush
My eyes were clear my lips untouched

I remember days of yore
The future held all things in store
The mysteries of each passing day
When love unused and silent lay

Upon the heart a gift to give
It seemed a purpose just to live
That was before the knowledge came
That love was just a cruel game

When hearts could break with just a thought
And could not heal although we sought
In tears and pain that could not tell
When time would heal and all is well

And still in future days align
The heart aware in its design
The road ahead no flowers grow
But only show the way to go

TO A MEMORY

I held you in my loving arms
For such a little while
I pictured you a grown up man
But lost you as a child

And even though that time as passed
It seems like yesterday
I see you now in memory
You're not so far away

I can close my eyes right now
And see your dear sweet face
And dream that you are here again
And live within that state

Your leaving served no purpose
Within my aching heart
The years gone by it seems to me
We never are apart

This aching haunts my memories
They keep your presence near
It's love that holds you close in time
In love your everywhere

PRAYING

As she knelt with fingers touching
Pointed to the sky
She spoke of troubles, broken dreams
And often asked God why
No doubt she had been trying
As she worked each given day
Sometimes her heart was heavy
And there were no words to say
There in the fading twilight
And still upon her knees
In the silence of her vigil
In the whisper of the trees
The chirping of the night birds
As they settled in to rest
And saw another dying day
With splendor in the west
And as she lay her weary head
Upon the counterpane
She knew that on the morrow
The sun would rise again
The hawk would get the night bird
The wind could fell the tree
And God would hear her prayer of thanks
For all that's meant to be

THE LADY OF THE LAMP

She, a vague shadow of my past
Heard a call from God while still a lass
A smouldering ember deep within her heart
To lay, to fester, from the want to start
But not to please herself, for fame or wealth
And not because of strength or health
An urgent dream did torture and did stay
To give herself for good did yearnings lay
And time would pass in anguish spent
Years that bid no pleasure but torment
Before the time did almost take its toll
This lass will heed her heart and soul
God will lead those who will be led
She heard this inner voice that said
Take up the lamp and lead the way
For those who stumbled in the dark each day
And make the living easier to bear
And gentle death for those who fear
Her hand held out to all who were in need
With strength from God would this lass lead
Forward through the decades she would go
Though days and nights not gently flow
But press the soul and hurt the heart
With all this pent up energy to start

Not daunted from the pressures from without
Within did battle frustration fear and doubt
But held the lamp for all to see
As if it were a magic key
And those who knew no hope till then
Turned fear to joy and boys to men
And busy years would come and die
Her tears would water where they lie
These wasted souls that saw the light
That shone awhile through deaths dark night
But none would leave her presence, die or live
Who did not feel her will to give?
And years would steal her days and lie
But still she held her lamp on high
For courage kept the tiny flame
And all in need would speak her name
Now in the blackness of the sky
Her tiny lamp is seen on high
And speaks of courage whence it came
As no man will forget her name
Florence nightingale

NOISY LOVE

I am a noisy love I know
I yell it loud I tell him so
His love is quiet as can be
He never says that he loves me
So I assume, sometimes pretend
His love's so great it has no end
But still behind my heart I feel
An aching spot that won't quite heal
I need the salve of loving words
From some romantic song I've heard
To put this aching heart to rest
He knows the words I like the best
Some unseen something to hold close
The part of love I like the most

MEMORIE LANE

There's nothing I like better
Than walking down memory lane
Looking at pictures of long ago
Hearing an old refrain
Even if they stir in my heart
A longing I can't explain
I see the past it's all I ask
When I walk down memory lane
Sometimes it brings me sweet sweet joy
Sometimes it brings me pain
Sometimes I have to be so brave
Walking down memory lane
It's a place of mixed emotion
That's in a different strain
Pictures fused in different hues
This walk down memory lane
And someday when the longing comes to me
You will probably find me again
With my treasure chest and the things I like best
Walking down memory lane

MY CHILDRENS WAY

Roads in different directions
Only in visual distance
Out of reach except emotionally
But can be touched at a glance

Only verbal help I offer
From my experience store
I see the pitfalls far ahead
And watch them evermore

And they in turn will feel this pain
When they look back like I
And see their lives again repeat
Mistakes and wonder why

When will it change or is each year
Preprinted in the mind
The road we walk past footsteps trod
All ready predefined

A guiding hand from out the past
All settled all arranged
So we just live our destiny
And nothing can be changed

MY DOMAIN

I sat in my garden and I said to me
I've smelt all the flowers, sat under my tree

I dug in the ground and planted a seed
It's been a good day a good day indeed

The birds have been hear since the first light of dawn
They`ve splashed in my bird bath they've sat on my lawn

I lounged in my chair all warm and content
And thrilled to the core with each new event

But now that I think this was my dream
My life every day to be peaches and cream

And I'm thankful to God for everything here
As I view my domain from my cozy chair

PRARIE ROSE

Lay me for my last sleep
Where the wind may blow and moan
And pick the fragrant prairie rose
To rest against the stone

No thoughts of earthly duty
I am no more of thee
I feed and enter into
The prairie rose and tree

DIFFERENT ROAD

The road not taken comes to mind
When quiet times prevail
A walk in dream like trance
That far elusive trail

And matched each step for step in time
The choices left to lie
And untouched life so still and dead
As time goes by

Life does not say what might have been
Or what may now befall
As time goes by and marks each day
Not ours to recall

CHILDHOOD

I brought with me from childhood
The little lass I was
I kept her with me deep inside
And that was good because
The days I traveled needed light
The time was dark and long
And so she brought me happiness
Her memory was strong

The need for her sustained me
I could my thoughts arrange
To enter in and find delight
In every childhood game
She took me back to yesterday
As memories will last
I lived it over once again
The childhood of my past

LONELY ROAD

There is a spot inside of me
Neglected and alone
And fading to a distant past
Becomes a distant moan
And I am losing sight of me
As apathy will reign
And like a vapor fading fast
May never come again
The winds of time blow softer now
And cool the savage breast
The fire of ambitions
Are finally laid to rest
And I have passed the times to turn
To grasp and hold to hand
The music of my early life
To hear my marching band
Day by day of marking time
Accepting as my load
No signpost helps this traveler
Along life's lonely road

THE GIFT

Days full of flowers
A dawn full of dew
Days full of memories
And thinking of you

Time when no sadness
Touches my heart
When all of life's worries
Just seem to depart

And I float on a cloud
In a world of my own
When all is good work
And I'm not all alone

But part of life's mysteries
And part of life's plan
Like a gift from the Gods
Not shown to all man

SPIN OUR YEARS

Days each lie in wait
To take our time
To spin our years
Yours and mine

The plans we have in head and heart
Are changed as minutes fly
As if we had no will at all
We watch the time go by

But still we plan the years ahead
As if in this we see
Our dreams emerge
And thus take shape in to reality

We must push forth
If life is changed, complete
We try to learn a lesson
With mistakes that we repeat

We try and try, for this is life
We live what we believe
We rectify our days in years
And thus we may achieve

NATURE

Sunbeams and daisies I see on my way
In the soft gentle breezes they gracefully sway
And I've learned something just at a glance
That daisies with breezes can curtsy and dance

I learned that the squirrel is smarter than I
And humming birds hover and back up when they fly
And water I see though it does not have feet
Can run down the gutter and out to the street

And leaves change their color without any paint
And fall off the tree as if in a faint
And scurry along faster than me
And some are still watching up in the tree

The trees that's grown tall with their heads in the clouds
Can rustle and groan like there laughing out loud
A spider can spin a doily of lace
And dance on the surface with rhythm and grace

All of nature when you look gives a sign
Were in this together, so keep it in mind

OLD SAINT NICK

I can't believe it's Christmas time
It came again so quick
But I have hung the stockings up
Now waiting for Old Nick
My kitchen's full of Christmas smells
Like my meat pie and cake
And sugar cookies green and red
And all the things I bake
I hear the Christmas hymns I love
I smell the standing pine
And welcome friends and family
For one whole day they're mine
The children's faces all aglow
They're eyes like shining stars
The books and dolls for little girls
And boys with games and cars
And finally the day is spent
I'm bathed in Christmas afterglow
And old Saint Nick just did the trick
Beneath the scented pine
I got the thing I wanted most
For one whole day they're mine

JACK

I remember when it rained
We use to stay inside
And when it thundered I was scared
But you were at my side

I remember that you made
A little wooden cart
With just a box and carriage wheels
And the goodness of your heart

I remember silver sands
And Sunday picnics to
I remember how I felt
And all because of you

Some sad some happy times
Memories hard to shake
All of these are feelings
It took the years to make

MY BROTHER

A girl just needs a brother
To fill her childhood years
To lift her up when she falls down
To wipe away her tears

To make her days go easy
To fill with laughter too
Each tiny corner of her heart
With happy things to do

As underneath the lamppost
We played each childhood game
Like hide and seek and kick the can
And some without a name

And picnicked on a Sunday
With family and friends
I feel the sand between my toes
The memories have no end

And when I take the time to dream
It seems like yesterday
The love I feel is still the same
And never goes away

MOTHER IN MY MIIND

I saw her head was nodding
Still the needle in her hand
As she neatly filled each stocking toe
As she wove each tiny strand

And I thought of all the working
As I slipped it in my shoe
Do other mothers mend each sock?
Like mother used to do

I felt the cozy cross-stitch patch
My slipper sought to hide
The feel of it filled loneliness
Kept mother at my side

And though no one could see it
My pride would keep from view
I'd rather have that mended sock
I would not trade for new

For with each cherished memory
The good old fashioned kind
All the things she did for me
Kept mother in my mind

ASPIRE

I see great trees in autumn mode
They turn their leaves to autumn gold
Nature knows the reason why
They shed their leaves but do not die

But return again in spring
To house the nest of birds on wing
They share their beauty grace the eye
And reach to touch the new spring sky

They seem to dance with style and grace
They seem to know their seasons place
Do not aspire or fret like me
They're happy just to be a tree

THE GIRL I USED TO BE

I dare not think of yesterday
It tears my heart asunder
Where memory plays games with me
And makes me think and wonder

And I am prone to pictures
That pass from mind to eye
And fill my throat with ushered tears
Before they fade and die

When day is done and shadows fall
And I am all alone
I start to fill the bygone days
My memories will roam

And though I'm courting danger
And thoughts are scattered free
I see someone familiar
The girl I used to be

THE SPARK

He's not here, but he's not gone
He's in my heart and there he stays
A heavenly love a love beyond
These worldly times these worldly ways

Sometimes love is close to death
But memories will give that glow
To relight love to start anew
When the lamp of faith is burning low

The winds of time can fan a spark
So close to dead but amber glow
Will come alive and start a flame
To warm the heart as lovers know

For love has many facets
And even left for dead
It comes alive and longs to live
With just a word that lovers said

The life of love includes the pain
There is no guarantee
But time and tears will work it out
For you and me

TRULY MINE

I can pretend you love me
Though tears are in my eyes
I can remember how it was
Before the love had died

I can pretend that you are here
I smell your aftershave
I remember sweet goodbyes
Your kisses and your waves

I wait for evening time to call
My time or it would seem
For then again you're truly mine
When I lie down and dream

GRAMMAS HOUSE

Gramma keeps cookies in cans on the shelf
She does not keep cookies in cans for herself
They're special surprises that she calls a treat
And they're only for special young people to eat
Gramma has beds that are soft as can be
With colorful quilts just so that we
Can snuggle and burrow a place that's just right
To sleep and to dream all the rest of the night
And my dreams are of cookies in cans on the shelf
And I dream that my gramma says, "Please help yourself"

DYING LOVE

Why is it that the ones we love
Can never fill our needs
We plant the seeds of loves neglect
With reckless thoughts and deeds

As unknowingly we squander
Loves times with empty thought
And never know the words we spend
Are what the years have bought

To look ahead we only see
The need to fill our heart
And think the time will last and last
And be just like the start

And now we live with hearts that ache
And fires that we can't mend
For hindsight is cold comfort
At the end

HEAR THE DARK

There is a place of deep despair
Where dead dreams and tears and misery fare
No doors open no soft voice will call
No kisses or hugs or memories at all

And time there is pain and agonies glean
And blackness devours till morning is seen
But then all the memories of past hours spent
Come back on a flood each painful event

When twilight descends and misery will make
The blackest of hours come back to awake
And play on my heart and force me to woo
Each feeling and thought and dead dreams anew

When will the pain of each day disappear?
If I don't hold the memory so tight or so near
They say that in time when I look back and see
The far distant past never happened to be
I hear what they say but it won't touch my heart
For I see the twilight and I hear the dark

GENTLE ALL THE WHILE

Just a baby grown tall
She does not know the world at all
She sees no shadows standing near
She feels no trepidation, fear

And friend to everyone she meets
A smile to everyone she greets
She practices loving everyday
A hand to all along the way

And when the winds of time blow cold
As she is moving on to old
Even then she'll find a smile
As she is gentle all the while

THE SMILE

I remember you were little
I did not think you'd grow
So big so tall so fast
Into someone I do not know

There is no trace of little
In the man that's standing there
Someone erased the little
And taken him somewhere

A mother has the patient love
To dream and wait awhile
And then remember little
When she sees the big man smile

SUMMER CAME ON STOCKING FEET

When I am down in deep despair
I look at trees and know that there
Are waiting buds all new unseen
That turn the lovely tree to green

For summer came on stocking feet
And did not herald falls defeat
But stirred and grew with wild abound
And there was beauty all around

And in my heart a joyous leap
As flowers, trees awake from sleep
And I again rejoice to start
And grow a garden in my heart

LOVE

The hearts a home where love resides
It's never coy, it never hides
It's past it's future and beyond
And always true when called upon

Love is like a golden cape
The warmth the shine when first awake
To hold the heart and show the way
Two loves together every day

The scent of love is like a rose
It lingers on in deep repose
And ever true and ever kind
Because it's never out of mind

THE SILVER ROAD

The silver road stretched straight ahead
And beckoned to my mind
I followed on the silver road
And left the earth behind

And it was so beguiling
It wrapped me in it's light
As moonbeams liquid fingers
Reached from the velvet night

And far to late I realized
I was alone and lost
And I looked back with longing
As I was torn and tossed

My earthly woes forgotten
In my struggle to survive
There was nothing I could hold to
As I floated with the tide

And I would end as flotsam
Like shells upon the beach
And follow on the silver road
Till life was out of reach

SEEKING

Just a tiny little spot
To keep the world at bay
A time to sit and contemplate
A sorting if we may

A touching of the shadows
To figure out and find
A reaching for a truer self
Deep down within the mind

And we may in our striving
Find an inner peace
By sorting out our pain and woe
And giving it release

And walking on a new path
Accepting nothing less
We may reach a state of mind
Of joy and happiness

MY LIFE

What would I do with my life?
If I did not have a broom
How would the minutes go?
If I did not cook at noon
What would fill my ears?
If the washer did not turn
If I did not stand beside the stove
To see that things don't burn

How would I spend my day?
When I am all alone
Except to plan for loved ones
And wait to see them home
And even though my daily tasks
Will fill my time each day
What would I be, how would I live
If they all went away

TEARS INSIDE

There's times I feel I need to cry
Some days I do not know just why
I feel as if I touch a place
That needs the tears upon my face

My throat all tightened up with fear
That seems to catch me unaware
And I am covered up with pain
As I remember once again

A memory of the days gone by
Of things that make me want to cry
And though I told my heart to stay
And try its strength to pass the day

I find I am not in command
To use my strength to take a stand
But let my feelings overflow
And take my heart where it will go

Until I am but shadows gray
That float unnoticed through the day
Tomorrow comes without a care
And eyes are dry without a tear
But here the future still resides
With memories and tears inside

THE LURKS

In the shadow world of come and go
Of push and pull, of yes and no
Live creatures that you cannot see
They do not look like you and me
But still they like to play and work
But what they do the best is lurk
Sometimes if you look very fast
You'll see a movement going past
A tiny step a squeak a sound
Just as you start to turn around
A pebble moves within the brook
And maybe if you stop to look
You'll see the little pebbles fly
But do not even blink your eye
Where do you think the flowers go?
Or soft winds when they cease to blow
The thoughts you think of in your mind
And things that are so hard to find
Lost books and clothes sometimes a ball
Maybe they are not lost at all
But borrowed by the lurking ones
They take them all, but just in fun

MUDDLED

I was feeling quite rejected
By the things my dreams suggest
Jumbled twisted without sense
Leaving me befuddled, dense
But who am I to seek and find
The wisdom in a dream defined
And pluck the very grain of thought
That smarter wisdom seekers sought
And make the days ahead give me
Those precious visions that I see
And yet when dark takes over day
I know that dreams will have their way
To show me things I can't define
To test my very soul and mind
And show the truth I can't ignore
That I'm no smarter than before
It seems that dreams just tell us lies
And leave us thoughts that tantalize
With hidden tricks and murky signs
They show us roads that twist and wind
And seem to have no destination
But leave us full of aggravation
It is the essence that it takes
To face our life when we're awake

Hilda Nightingale

MY LITTLE PATCH OF GREEN

A little patch of green grass
A tree or two or more
All hidden by a trellis fence
Behind a garden door

The flowers safe and blooming
Some dancing too and fro
Some left for heavens garden
And others left to grow

So thus we pass the season
My little patch and I
Together caring sharing
We watch the season fly

I look into the future
And know that it will bring
The joy of this my garden
That comes to me each spring

LILAC MEMORY

The lilac lane floods back to hold
The scent of days of yore
The lilac lane that leads me back
Up to a cottage door

And I am lost in memory
It fills my heart and mind
I hold this special picture
To warm the passing time

I do not miss today at all
For I am warm in thought
When lilacs make me misty eyed
And memories are caught

Upon a passage deep in time
Where I am wont to dwell
If only for a little while
For in a dream like spell

We savor special moments sent
To help us on our way
The lilac lane floods back again
To warm me every day

THE TREES

Thank you mighty trees for shade
You're a treat for tired eyes
I know within your limbs are nests
For hidden birds with hidden cries

You are such a pretty sight
Your rough brown coat and leaves of lace
You tease and taunt me as I lay
With shadow notes upon my face

Conducting earths tunes as you bend
Dancing in the evening breeze
I will hold it in my heart
This ballet of the trees

TWO BY FOUR DOMAIN

Under the kitchen table
With the flowered oilcloth floor
I have a little place to hide
With a blanket for a door

I'm alone where I want to be
Marching to my band
I hear the rain on the window
In some far off distant land

And the swish and sway of the corn broom
Used by a giants hand
And now there's only here and now
No memories remain
Under the kitchen table
In my two by four domain

IF I MEET AN ANGEL

If I should meet an angel
How lucky I would be
Imagine if an angel
Showed herself to me
And maybe she would tell me
Places I should go
And whisper sweet things of life
That only angels know
We could be in a garden
Enjoying the flowers there
For angels know them all by name
That's growing everywhere
And angels talk to every bird
Direct them in their song
Each note they sing is true and sweet
No note is ever wrong
If I should meet an angel
Who will watch and help me grow
It could be someone really nice
That I already know

THANKS

My silence is a prayer to God
For he sees in my heart
All the things I want to say
That never get a start

My day is full of wondrous things
I want to thank Him for
And I can never find the words
But just ask Him for more

It's a feeling that just fills my time
And makes my life worthwhile
For He has given me His love
Since I was just a child

WE'LL MEET AGAIN

A gentle hand caressed my brow
In gentle eyes the fright
A gentle voice said please dear God
Don't take my love tonight

But I was longing for my home
And I had seen the sign
I closed my eyes and drifted forth
Her white head close to mine

I'll wait for you I whispered
In God's sweet loving grace
I heard her say sweet journey
As tears fell on my face

DREAMS

Dreams that never end are unfulfilled
But still the dreamers dream each day
And the years pass and die
And dreams are scattered on the way
Not noticed by the dreaming one
Their path is warm and straight ahead
They do not see with passing time
That some are worn and some are dead
And at the end of life and time
I would hope that they would see
Their battered dreams as sweet and clear
And clasp them close like me

MY CHILDREN

My own little sweet little children so dear
Remain in my memory year after year
And give me the warmth that I need every day
To follow my path, to follow my way
And what would I do if it wasn't for you
If I didn't have dreams of you what would I do
The day that shines bright, would be dull and grey
And flowers would wither and die on my way
For you are the nourishing force of my time
You are the purpose that makes my life rhyme
You make the love in my heart I hold near
My own little sweet little children so dear

IF I HAD KNOWN

If I had known, back years ago
God meant me to be me
The weary days just could have passed
As easy as can be
I could have let life lead me
Down a quiet worldly way
There would be no distractions
To let me go astray
I would not need to seek myself
For I was always here
I would not need to look for help
Or hope someone would care
It took me years, and almost all
My life to let me see
He thought me worthy all along
God meant me to be me

UNKNOWN DREAMS

We are shadows on the earth
And only to ourselves are real
Our thoughts are silent, dreams unknown
Our words forgotten less we kneel

When we are gone, never missed
Even if we're loved awhile
A fleeting thing this passion
A tiny memory, a smile

It's but a ghost in thought
To tantalize, then slip away
There is nothing left of me
That isn't back in yesterday

YESTERDAY

Don't close the door on yesterday
And all the beauty there
For it sustains me everyday
I want to keep it near

The childhood times when looking back
Feeds my heart and soul
And sits more dearer every day
Now I'm growing old

I compare those times with these
And find today I lack
The closeness and security
So I keep looking back

I pity youth that see no ties
For in their time ahead
They'll pay for every thought and deed
For every word they said

And there will be no comfort
No looking back on these
The deeds and dreams of yesterday
That make our memories

THIS IS A MEMORY

Yesterday, gone, used up
A page in a diary, a thought

A regret, a tear,
All the days and hopes of a year

Pushed behind today, and forgotten
Until we need a moment to remember
A nice thing that happened last September

And then all the hours flood back
To hurt, make us laugh, smile
And to warm us for awhile

VIRTUE

If every year is measured
By the treasures that we keep
And every day is thought as good
By conquests that we reap
And we only see the value
In what we have at hand
And we work each day, just for the coin
That's always in demand
Then we lose sight of living
And our time is spent in vain
As we use our days for gathering
That's all we ever gain
We won't broaden our horizon
Or enlarge our mind to see
We remain so small and narrow
And that's all we'll ever be
For in our daily living
If we don't take time to grow
How will we learn about the world
How will we ever know

That a butterfly can rest with ease
Upon a daisy's head
How will we see the mother bird
And how her babies fed
Or watch a maple shed her leaves
All crimson red in fall
Or see the sunset in the west
Then hear a night bird call
Or lend a hand to someone
And learn to fill a need
To overcome our selfishness
Our avarice and greed
We cannot live with grasping hand
Or each day by the sword
But we must live with trust and hope
For our reward

HOME AT LAST

The angels looked from heaven, saw her here
They saw how sweet she was, and held her dear
I understood just why they came
And called my darling home, by name
They took her hand, this little lass
To silver trees and golden grass
And I was left alone in dark despair
Still seeing her sweet face, and shining hair
And pain is all I know, but it will pass
When I see silver trees, and golden grass

A LITTLE GIRL

When I was just a little girl
My daddy went away
It hurt me awful deep inside
I didn't want to play

I thought that I had done some wrong
I thought I had been bad
For other little girls I knew
Had both a mom and dad

There's lots of things a kid can miss
When they are very small
It seemed to be a waiting time
A time I would recall

That hidden, missing, something
That kept my heart aware
The outside just pretended
There was no inside fear

The years have left me tall and sad
And much against my will
I find with pain, and silent tears
That I am waiting still

THE HILLS

I look to the west at the close of day
As the sun slips behind a hill
And I watch the colors that fuse the sky
As everything grows still
And the rosy glow turns to purple
And then to a midnight blue
And silhouettes the edge of my world
And the hills I thought I knew
And it fills my eye with beauty
And it fills my soul with song
The words lay quiet in my heart
But I hear them all night long
And memory bids me look again
To replenish my starving eye
And I watch, till the night takes over
And lights each star in the sky

TROUBLED MIND

I do not search my troubled mind
I could not be so brave
Because the past is hidden there
All things both sad and grave

And in the corners, in the dark
Past things I have forgot
Regrets, dead loves, and bitter words
And things that hurt a lot

So I've devised a way of life
That seems to fit my need
I laugh a lot, and keep it light
This way I do not heed

When there are times this does not work
When things don't turn out right
Some times when I am all alone
And in the dead of night

Then I must face my true self
These times I cannot lie
I see myself for what I am
And lie alone and cry

But when the morning turns to day
I smile, with head held high
You'd never know I can't forget
That lonesome by and by

KIND WORDS OF LOVE

There could be love
If we didn't hold the hand of deep despair
If kind words had been spoken
And grey unhappy shadows disappear
There could be love if we could reach each other
A thought that drifts across the many miles
There could be love
If feelings did not hide
But spoke our minds in loving words
And lose our pride
There could be love
That's hidden now behind
The burdens that we carry
That makes love so very hard to find
There could be love
If we hear the message in the bluebirds song
And as the whisper of the summer breeze, sighs love
Then nothing would be wrong

THERE COULD BE LOVE

Would you see me as I am?
Not, what I know you wish of me
You would not stop and talk awhile
You would not turn the golden key
You would not hear my calling voice
Or feel my hand to fill your own
I am sure, you would pass by
And both of us would walk alone
We would not feel our spirits blend
I would not fill a special need
You would not feel my racing pulse
We would not share the blessed seed
But one of us may feel the loss
And hear the breaking of a heart
For there is pain, and there are tears
When love does not, take time to start

INTO LIFE'S STREAM

Into life's swift stream we stride
With nothing but our hopes to guide
Clutching straws as they float by
Bumping jagged rocks that lie
To catch us as we labour on
Sand bars of days were caught upon
And in the end an ocean wide
With just our broken dreams to guide
And nothing firm to keep afloat
If we have lost our faith and hope
We need a rudder straight and true
Some one who cares to be our crew
A vision of a distant shore
Some place we have been searching for
Our journey may be just a day
As we anchor in some restful bay

THE OLD TRUNK

A photograph, a book or two
Marked at a certain page
A feathered hat that's flat and worn
That used to be the rage
A flower pressed, and brown with time
A dress that's out of style
Put in the trunk to keep
For just a little while
And in the spring at cleanup time
I sort out lovingly
And find I cannot throw away
What means so much to me

FLUSH AWAY

I wish that the people, at night, would refrain
From flushing the water, that goes down the drain
For then I awake, and lay there and stare
At the ceiling, till dawn and I don't think it's fair
It runs through the pipes like Niagara Falls
And echoes on floors, and ceilings, and walls
And as it retreats to a murmur or two
It happens again, with somebody new
And as dawn brings the rush
And I hear the birds peep
That's the time my eyes close
But it's too late to sleep

SOMEONE REMEMBERS

The battle years had marred the fields
The trees are long since dead
As are the sons of many men
No crosses where they bled

The wind that blew around me there
Did sob and sigh and wail
As if to me, communicate
The sorrow of the tale

As time had passed, I chanced to stop
To pray and bow my head
The battle field was covered with
A snow white daisy bed

IN THE CORNER OF MY GARDEN

In the corner of my garden
There's a little place I know
And I like to go and rest there
When the sun is setting low
I like to just sit back there
Sit back and rest my feet
And let memories have their way
The memories oh so sweet
Sometimes they bring me laughter
Sometimes they bring a tear
Sometimes they are so beautiful
It's all that I can bear
And when the waning sun
Slips low behind the hill
And evening time comes courting
And everything is still
Oh how I love my garden
With that little place I know
And when sorrow steals the happy times
This is where I go

A TRIP TO MACAROON ALLEY

Little Joey left home today
To macaroon alley across the way
He wanted to see the world, he did
But Joey was just a little kid
And didn't know how big and wide
The world can be, when you're outside
Up to now he had only seen
The outside world through the back door screen
So he took his grandma's rocking chair
Because he saw it sitting there
And he rocked down the alley as fast as he could
He'd see the whole world, he would, he would
And as he went he said a rhyme
"I have to be home by supper time
Cause we're having goom by slish"
And this was Joey's favourite dish
Joey met Romper and he said, "Hey"
"Where do you think you're rocking today?"
"To see the world and I must go
I have to be home for supper you know
Cause we're having goom by slish
And that's my very favourite dish"

Now Joey could see a light ahead
"It must be the end of the alley," he said
"I wonder what color the world will be?"
And Joey could hardly wait to see
As Joey rocked on he saw a gate
Maybe the world will have to wait
But he rocked up close
And he stared real hard
Why the world looked the same as his own backyard
So Joey rocked home, singing his rhyme
"I have to be home by supper time"
His mother filled up a big red dish
And Joey ate all of his goom by slish

DAISY DOODLE'S WALK

Little Daisy Doodle went walking in the wood
She went to find a Leprechaun; at least she thought she could
For she knew that he was Irish, and she knew that he was green
And he was very tiny, and hardly ever seen
Little Daisy Doodle walked till it was dark
And finally knew that she was lost, and stopped to ask a lark
If he could please direct her, to the village on the hill
He said he didn't know the way, but chipmunk probably will
"Where will I find the chipmunk?" Daisy Doodle said
"He lives up in the meadow, about a mile ahead
Right beside the old oak tree, beside the running brook
If you do not hear him, all you have to do is look."
Little Daisy Doodle didn't want to fret or weep
She saw that it was getting dark, and everyone's asleep
But she hurried, how she hurried, as quickly as she could
And she stumbled and she faltered as she hurried through the wood
"Maybe," said Daisy Doodle "If I hum a little song,
The way won't be so scary; the way won't be so long"

She took a breath and started on a song she used to know
A song about a little girl, it started sweet and low
And so she sang it loudly, as if her heart would break
She filled her ear and heart with song, the forest came awake
And an angry squirrel chattered, and scolded, "Don't you know,
its night time and I'm sleepy, will you hurry up and go?"
And a bluebird sang a song slightly out of tune
"I only sing songs sweetly, when it's getting close to noon."
Daisy saw a clearing, and there before her eyes
Stood a lovely lady all in white, she looked both kind and wise
She said, "I am the finder of both girls and boys
I also help find lost things, like dolls, and dogs, and toys
But no one ever sees me, except a time or two
When someone sings sweet and low, and then I come to view
I come to those that have lost heart, and those that lose their way
One time, oh it was long ago, I found the month of May
Now close your eyes, and dream real hard." That's what the lady said
And Daisy Doodle closed her eyes, and woke up home in bed

THE VACANT HOUSE

Where have they gone?
All those who's laughter rang within my walls
I look with eyes of glass
At empty rooms and vacant halls
Sad flowers beside unused paths
Wind whispering in dry leaves
No fire warms these empty rooms
But chimneys filled with nests, the swallows weave
I remember laughter and love
Tears and sadness too
That made up life down through the years
I watched them as they grew
And hope will spring eternal
I listen for the gate
But no one comes to warm this hearth
But still I wait…

THE PREACHER

When I heard the preacher speak
As I settled in the pew
I was filled with dedication
And I knew what I should do
Embrace the world, its people
Take on their pain and woe
Do good in word, do good in deed
Pick up the cross and go
And how the spirit rose in me
It filled my heart and soul
I pictured all my days ahead
With goodness as my goal
And as the hymns were sung
My vision floated high
I saw the good works, I would do
Each day before I die
And oh the inspiration
The sacrifice and pain
Why I would give up everything
For what I had to gain
And as I left the church that morn
And shook the preacher's hand
I marched ahead with steady step
To join the hopeful band
It wasn't too far from the church
I met with apathy
It said there is tomorrow
And I returned to me

A FAMILY

I remember yesterday
When brooks were clear and sometimes blue
I remember yesterday
The air was sweet and each day started clean and new
I remember yesterday
When smiles were shared and steps were slow
I remember yesterday
All we met were friends and few we did not know
We were closer then, to what God meant us all to be
A family of his children and one humanity

COME DANCE FOR ME

Come dance for me
In your dress of gold
Come dance for me
And warm me when I'm cold
Though I may be alone
The lonesome will depart
For you will gladden
All my minutes and my heart
I see your steps
Each in shining light
Choreographed by no man
Graceful in the black of night
The hours I sit and dream
Not to depart in haste
When I watch you dance
Upon a log, within my fireplace

MYSTERY

That's the way it goes, this other state
That shadowed world, where things are late
And always undecided, and unsure
Behind that blank unopened door
It happens when we are alone
These happenings we can't condone
And many times if you look fast
You'll see a movement that has passed
A tiny step, a squeak, a sound
Just as you start to turn around
And, one day, when you take pause
To ponder on, to find the cause
It's wasted time, because I know
I just accepted long ago
And blame it on a gnome or elf
Or something you have done yourself
It's happened down through history
So just enjoy the mystery

SHARING

True love will last forever
If love will keep by caring
But love is only half
For love is in the sharing
Like a golden band
Two loves are intertwined
And like the purest gold
The years, this love refined
Until its shining light
Surrounds us every day
And we are one with all the world
As our love lights the way
No matter where we go
We are forever wrapped
In loves soft golden glow

AS THE DAY IS DYING

Just as the day is dying
It sheds its rosy glow
And paints all things before my eye
And changes what I know

It glints against the window pane
And sparkles in the grass
Then gives an eerie half light
Before the hours pass

And as the day is folding
An evening takes her place
They merge into half shadows
Grey velvet and rose lace

And all things seem suspended
Decisions not quite made
To push the day behind it
Before the night is laid

And I must wait expectant
For I can do no less
The stars and moon take over
When the day is laid to rest

NATURES WAY

Days are lived and go
That's how we live and grow
As time is spent in each pursuit
And every minute bears new fruit
Some sweet, some bitter, and indeed
The product of the planted seed
We sow each day and year of time
The daily deeds return in kind
And so we harvest happiness
Despair and pain if we transgress
We're born to follow nature's way
Or we must pay

AS MEANT TO BE

There are windows in my dreams
For I don't live alone
So I pull shades to close them out
No interfering telephone
I softly close my tired eyes
To soft grey mist, a violet hue
But only for a little while
To let my dreams pass in review
For I must finally raise the shades
And let in cold reality
Accept my days, the road ahead and see
Life as it's meant to be

BACK THEN

I won't go back, because I know
I did it once, sometime ago
And all the things when I was small
Were changed, or were not there at all
The tree I loved, they had cut down
I did not recognize the town
My school that stood so grand and tall
Is now a busy shopping mall
And all that had sustained me when
I searched my memories, and then
Reflected on what made me grow
To be the person that you know
Who journeyed back to view the past
Found only memories will last
For what we had and used to be
Will all be changed, if now we see
Behind us, it's not there at all
We should not heed that backward call
But trust our dreams, and look ahead
For yesterday is truly dead

THE WONDER

I wonder where the wonder went
For when I was a child
It shone like gold in all I saw
A promise all the while
Each year brought new surprises
A miracle each day
And filled my heart with wonder
As I skipped along the way
But shadows crept along the years
And chill winds blew despair
I lost the wonder of those times
I couldn't find it anywhere
But as I grew with time and thought
As wisdom changed my mind
A childlike splendour filled my days
It wasn't hard to find
For it had hidden in my heart
And waited there content
Until I took the time to find
Just where the wonder went

A WORD

A careless word can hurt the heart
And sometimes make the tear drops start
And spoil a day and lose a friend
And leave us lonely in the end

If only we would think awhile
The words we say so sharp with guile
Retract and change to something nice
Not speak, before we think it twice

We'd make someone a happy day
Not chase some new found friend away
Good words are like the sun, they heal
They bless the heart, and make us feel

So at the start, if we but learn
That what we say, in part return
And color us for all to see
They weave our personality

COMPETITION

I need to know you care for me
Each time that you are near
A little touch, a small caress
Your fingers in my hair
For love to me is verbal
I need the words you say
To let me know you really care
Each and every day
My life is fed on feelings
I cannot just survive
With thoughts that maybe you still care
So each day I contrive
To flaunt myself, to preen and flounce
And hope you will see me
But alas, it's all in vain
You're watching our T.V.

MY DREAM WORLD

My dream world is warm and wonderful
I go there every day
When ever I am sad and blue
And I can steal away

It's everything that it can be
To warm my heart and mind
It's soft sweet music to the ear
Its candlelight and wine

It's mauve pink twilight, fading
Then light by silver star
Just passed the promise of the sun
Tomorrow stretching far

My time is full of feeling
As quiet moments pass
I live a lifetime every one
As precious as the last

Then back into the rude world
With pain and sorrow laced
For I must live the life in which
I have been placed

THE POLKA DOT TIE

I met an alligator green
It was the very first I'd seen
I heard him slurp, and crunch, and munch
For he was sitting down to lunch
Upon a man who just passed by
Who wore a red and yellow tie
And! He didn't tell me that
He ate his shoes, his suit, his hat
Nor would he even tell me why
He ate it all except the tie
The red and yellow polka dot
I would have thought, he'd eat the lot
He let me go for I was late
And he was full, because he ate
And as I pondered on my way
He waddled off, and said good day
Another day I chanced to spot
A red and yellow polka dot
Around the neck of gator green
And now he looked so trim and lean
He didn't have a shirt or vest
But just the tie, he ate the rest
And then I knew the reason why
He did not want to eat the tie
It wasn't that it made him ill
But that it made him dressed to kill

WITH FAITH

Betrayed by hope, that always springs eternal
In the hearts of those who reach for the stars
And learn no lesson in they're failure
Using the dawn to launch new dreams
Wearing their days proudly
Hiding there disappointment in the night
Turning their faces to the sky, with anticipation, and a smile
And moving forward

GREEN MEADOWS

I see a soft green meadow in my mind
It tempts my very soul to go and stay
So I play truant with my fading time
Forget the passing minutes of the day

But even as I pause to rest, reflect
I feel the call of works I've left undone
And plagued with all of yesterday's neglect
That should be seen before another sun

I must return, and leave this pleasant place
For it does not exist, except in mind
Made up of gentle thoughts, and kindly views
This place that is so very hard to find

And only weary travellers will see
The soft green meadow of a future day
With all the dreams and hopes there is to be
And find that they may go, but never stay

No matter how we strive to be content
Our times allotted, gay and sad to each
We have to live each moment as it's sent
And find the soft green meadow out of reach

THEY DO NOT SEE

For all of those who will believe
Tomorrow never shows
And time is free to waste away
They think not where it goes
And words are markings in a book
And thoughts are held, and stilled
Good deeds are kept within the heart
And never gristed or milled
For all of those who don't feel life
Who do not laugh or cry
And do not see beyond themselves
They need not wait to die

QUIET TIMES

The dear sweet quiet times
I sit alone and think
I let the wonders I observe
Fill me like a drink
And quench my thirst for beauty
In my heart and soul
To cleanse my thoughts of fears
And make my life feel whole
The quiet noises fill my ear
And everything seems right
It lifts me from my lethargy
I see the starlit night
I need only moments spent
Tomorrow does not come to mind
I browse through thoughts of yesterday
Keeping only those I find
That please the moment, now I live
As I would like, and trouble naught
To follow paths my feet would find
Or pattern plans, as is my lot
I do not know myself, or care
To meet, embrace the other me
For I have lost myself to time
Allowed myself to wander free

GOD'S CALLING

Just take my hand and feel my love
That never goes away
And as I age that sweet sweet voice
Gets louder every day

And deep within my aging heart
I pause for just a while
To hear that voice so sweet and soft
Like when I was a child

And it had always been there
For all, and every year
It speaks upon the winds of time
That sweet voice everywhere

THE SEA

The sea stretched out before me
Too far for eyes to reach
Out like a giant counterpane
Tucked in about the beach
The moon cast silver shadows
Upon the moonlit bay
And tiny chips of stars dropped down
To light the mermaids way
The seas a jealous lover
It hides its treasures deep
Down in a sea green garden
Where buried sailors sleep
But oh, I love to hear its song
The rolling withdrawn cry
It will not tell me where it goes
I sit and wonder why
It fills me with a feeling
I cannot put to words
It makes me ponder on the cause
Of how my heart is stirred
It rocks me to a dreamland
With its swish and sway
I sit, and watch, and listen
Content to stay

SILVER BELLS

I hear silver bells in my garden
God has planted them there
I hear them ringing sweetly
In the soft night air
And all the flowers waken
And lift their voice in song
Carried by the evening breeze
Clear and proud and strong
For they unlike us mortals
Sing to God on high
They seem to know what they must do
And do not question why
They fill life with their beauty
They light each passing day
For every weary traveller
Passing by their way
And even when they're silent
As if on bended knees
The scent and sound of silver bells
Is carried on the breeze

SEE ME

Dear good Lord while you are there
See me full of deep despair
See me hunger see me yearn
See I have no way to turn
Lift this burden from my heart
Give my life a brand new start
Give my eyes a clearer view
Purpose in the things I do
Let my lips speak only good
Let my ears hear what they should
Let me see the wonders there
Let me be a creature rare
Let me walk in God like ways
All the minutes of my days

A POEM

A poem is a singing from the heart
A thought, a dream just waiting there to start
A story that just must be said
When thoughts and deep emotions wed
A poem is not hard to find
That forms from pictures in your mind
Of things you see along the way
The warp and weave of time and space
Experience will leave a trace
Like rainbows sharing sky with rain
And feelings that come back again, and again, and again

BELIEVING

It's not hard to believe
When you see the sun dance on a buttercup
It's not hard to believe
When the dawns silver mist is seen when you first get up
It's not hard to believe
When the tall trees sway in the rosy glow of the dying day
As we amble through gardens along the way
It's not hard to believe

It's not hard to believe
When your heart is light when you're safe and warm
In the dark of night when you're sure of love and all is right
It's not hard to believe
When you find the faith to carry on
With hope in your heart at each new dawn
It's not hard to believe

THE PRESENCE

If I asked you to my garden
Just to sip a cup and talk
And look upon the wonders God has wrought
Do you think that He would listen
Because we are so comfy
Or because we aren't in church, that He would not
As we look upon His wonders
With each different shape and hue
It's just like a cathedral
With a dome of crystal blue
Surely God would come and join us
For I feel His presence near
There's a gentle peace, a singing joy
Presiding everywhere

HELP ME PRAY

I kneel to pray, and love will fill my heart
But my mind will wander, before the praying starts
I think of all my worries and all there is to do
Then all my troubles creep right in, when I pray to you
I know dear Lord you see me, and know me like a book
For there are copies of myself, everywhere you look
But with all your gentle patience, in all you think and do
You wait for every sinner who wants to come to you
I know you walked beside me, the minute I was born
I know I'll have a place, unworthy though I be
You see the little goodness deep down inside of me
A little corner saved for me when day is done
A place for even me to rest when life is run
For I am lost without your help, so let me say
Dear Lord, please see me kneel, and help me pray

LIFE'S PUZZLE

We grasp happiness in little pieces, and put them together like a puzzle
Sometimes they don't fit, but we force them together to please
ourselves
Not really liking the all over picture, but then it's all the pieces we have,
so we pretend we don't notice
For happiness is an illusion, shown to us just once in a while
Like small shafts of sunlight, to warm our days

UNHAPPINESS

My heart has lost its wings
It cannot fly to the tree of happiness
My eyes have lost their sight to see beauty
My ears are closed and do not hear the winds song
I pass through night and day as a grey shadow
So quietly that I disturb no one

THE ECHO OF LOVE

Sticky fingers on my wall
Boots and jackets in the hall
And though I scold them and complain
I hope I see them there again
My home may be a busy place
With dusty feet and muddy face
With dolls and trucks upon the floor
I'll clean it up and ask for more
A house can be all neat and clean
Like pictures in a magazine
But oh how cold they really are
I'd rather have my home by far
The sound of voices in each room
Their presence will be gone too soon
I see the years ahead, and know
That I'll be lonesome when they go

EMPATHY

I see within the folks I meet
Eyes dim with daily care
An unseen hand will grip my heart
I feel I want to share
The worries, hurts, the anguish
That hides their smiles away
To bring it back from deep within
By something I might say
And I am filled with empathy
Their tears will scald my face
I feel the pain and loneliness
Of all the human race
If I can help one little bit
By lending heart or ear
I'll take your burdens for a while
Because you see I care

YOU

You inflict your thoughts on me
There's gloom in everything I see
I let depression lead the way
I let sadness start my day
Suspended is my happiness
Somewhere between the blue
When I let everything I think
Depend on you

Hilda Nightingale

THE DEAD SOLDIER

You see it made no difference
I gave my life in vain
To end all strife, to end all wars
But see they fight again
They cannot hear my calling voice
In the whisper of the breeze
Above the roar of heavy guns
But this dead soldier sees
How senseless is their struggle
For no war is ever won
With the coin of mother's sorrow
With the losing of a son
And for every soldier fallen
In the name of future peace
There's a lonely loved one waiting
Whose pain will never cease

LOST MINUTES

Time has taught I could have dealt
With minutes as they came my way
I could have stopped to see life's beauty
It was there for me each day
I could have taken time to smile
For I had lots of them to share
All the pleasures life can offer
Are just sitting waiting there
When my heart is full of loving
And my mind with blessings sent
I can still feel sorrow reaching
To paint my thoughts where minutes went

CHILDHOOD

The days drift by
I think of times when as a child
I wished the years would hurry, fly
So I could stand up tall
And understand it all
What happened to my childish dreams?
Somehow I left them all beyond
In a land of distant make believe
Of storybooks and magic wand

SWEET VOICE

I searched my days, I searched my heart
Way back where shadows lay
The nameless years have stolen all
The long forgotten days

And there was only dry and brown
Like flowers when they die
These imprints of a memory
As quiet as a sigh

And I have lost all I have been
I did not even know
This faded shadow of myself
This weariness and so

I stare ahead with clouded eyes
For fear I would lose track
Of where my years have led
And showed, there was no turning back

But deep within my yearning heart
I pause for just a while
I hear a voice so sweet and soft
Like when I was a child

Say take my hand and feel my love
That never goes away
And as I age that sweet sweet voice
Grows stronger every day

A POT OF GOLD

I searched the world for happiness
And found a pot of gold
I hugged it to my lonely heart
And never told a soul
It filled my eye with wonder
It brightened every day
I kept it all, just for myself
Gave none of it away
But the gold began to tarnish
As I kept it for my own
It did not grow or flourish
But weighed me like a stone
It took love to tell me
If I spread it far and wide
Then it would come full circle
That it would multiply
I spread the gold of Jesus' word
All bright and shiny new
It filled my heart and weary soul
As only good will do

THE KEY

I cried aloud, but no one heard
And the window was so high
I did not know just where I was
And filled with questions why
There's no release from padded walls
I try to no avail
And the little window, up so high
Has iron bars like jail
There was no mirror on the wall
To show me who I'd see
And nothing there that gave me peace
And nothing fitted me
Except the quiet all the time
And the fear it did invoke
It flowed into my empty ear
It fitted like a cloak
Then, just a tiny ray of light
Between the bars shone through
And filled my heart with shining hope
And then at last I knew
I felt the warmth of Jesus' love
My prison went away
He is the warden of my soul
The key, is when I pray

COPING

When I was young, the years ahead
Looked soft and warm and cosy
No black clouds covered up the sun
And everything was rosy
And in my teens, my path was straight
And flat, and smooth, and wide
My heart had never felt an ache
My eyes had never cried
But suddenly the winds of change
Blew all of this away
And days were full of sorrow
That seem to hurt and stay
And I with little practice
To cope with fear and pain
Would hide my head, and wait to see
The good times pass again
But on the sea of life
I could not change the tide
I could not sail around the rocks
It did no good to hide
The sea of life washed over me
And I like all mankind
Must learn to swim, to stay afloat
And keeping this in mind
Extracting little bits of good
From every new found day
Till the fear of my tomorrow went away

ACCEPTANCE

The years had grown a garden
And as she wandered through
She didn't plant the lovely rose
Or anything that grew
The sunlight on the shading tree
The whisper of the breeze
She could not take the credit
For anyone of these
But choices they were made
And deep within her heart
She felt contented, at the end
And no new dreams to start
The years that passed, forgotten
Her days are quiet now
She cupped the daisy in her hands
And kissed its yellow brow

TILL WE ARE FREE

Within my self, from hidden depths
Comes pain, and thoughts of life
Bewildering, with haunted dreams
And laced with joy and strife
And mixed therein the feel of hope
Of searching in past days
A glimmer now of what had been
Not bright, in shades of greys
And with the searching, feeling starts
And tears, and change of mind
As minutes alter attitudes
And leave the greys behind
And I will trust again, because
I cannot live with doubt
For in the distant past I see
What life is all about
And I have once again endured
The trial days of pain
And push them far back in my mind
But they will come again
As life repeats its messages
And those with wisdom see
That there is nothing else to have
Till we are free

COME BACK

What were the words you had to say
I didn't want to hear
What were the pictures in your eyes
That filled me so with fear

I spoke to fill the quiet time
And change all things I could
To show you that you needn't speak
And that I understood

And though unspoken, I could feel
You drifting far away
I see your empty image
And strive to make you stay

How lonely are the minutes now
And each are days of waste
Your thoughts and dreams and all of you
Are in some distant place

A place I cannot enter
For even I must know
No matter how I love you
There are places I can't go

I wait, a lonely vigil
And hope that you will see
How much I love, and how the past
Means all the world to me

WHAT HAS BECOME OF ME

When did my days of happy end
When years allotted me
Seemed shadows of some other time
Too vague to even see

And I a stranger stood to fill
A space I could not find
I even lost the pictured past
It would not come to mind

There was no yesterday for me
All memories were dead
I stored no promises or hope
In what strange voices said

And passing through each night and day
And gentle though they be
I serve no purpose, thus I think
What has become of me?

GOD'S GIFTS TO ME

Sitting on top of a sunlit hill
Counting the stars by night
Holding a baby warm and close
Seeing a bird in flight
Touching the dew on velvet rose
Walking a mossy lane
Feeling the stirring of life around
Seeing a friend again
Knowing, and caring, and being loved
Awareness of all I see
And counting my blessings every one
These are God's gifts to me

TOGETHER

With you I see the days ahead
Marching to a special band
Into the sunset of our time
Side by side and hand in hand

The road of life is long and hard
The days will trip us with its tears
The moments smile upon our face
Together living through the years

And as the twilight time descends
I hear our love songs sweet refrain
And I will dance with memory
Until we meet again

I WALK TO THE GATE

I walk to the gate, but I never go through
For I know what will happen, if ever I do

I look past the gate, I hear and I see
I don't want that sadness to ever touch me

I walk to the gate and gaze far away
I see all the misery that passes each day

And all of the people, and all of their sorrow
Outside of the gate, will be there tomorrow

THE OLD MAN

The old man sat and pondered
On the good old days of yore
And all that made his memories
The times that went before
And as he stirred the ashes
Of the days that were his past
The ghosts of times, and folks he knew
Would rise and seem to last
And were by far more real to him
In faded memory
Then quiet times around him now
And what they seemed to be
More real to him, those yesteryears
He lived them now each day
The dreams of what his life would be
Had never gone away
And a tiny smile would play around
His thin lips, as he aged
Forgotten were the trying times
And battles that he waged
And he walked among his memories
Just choosing those that pleased
The hurts, the pains, the sorrows
Discarding all of these
They lighted up the final walk
He did not ask life why
But gathered up his memories
And never said goodbye

I CALL YOU FRIEND

It's just because I like you
And you will always see
When I am sad and lonely
You are a friend to me

It's just because I need you
For we all need someone who
We tell our secret longings
The things we want to do

It's just because I trust you
I say what's in my heart
The things that hurt and make me sad
And make the tear drops start

It's just because you really care
For all the time you spend
To listen to, and help me out
That I call you my friend

THE BEST OF ME CAN'T DIE

The best of me can't die
It must reside someplace
With all life's wonders kept
Like in a state of grace

The good thoughts that I think
The good deeds that I do
The visions that I see
My dreams all bright and new

The hopes that I held dear
All things that I did right
Should shine to guide the way
If just a tiny light

The love within my heart
The nice things that I say
The best of me I show
To folks along the way

Why should my goodness die?
It should be someplace new
All soft and shiny bright
Like clean fresh morning dew

Maybe a twinkling star
Maybe that's where it goes
A crystal drop of dew
That rests upon a rose

A gentle summer breeze
The flowers where they lie
If just to give some hope
The best of me can't die

THESE HANDS

These here hands have done a lot
They've led through life a tiny tot
They've stroked a head
They've made a bed
With gentle love they've held a babe
When worried they have often prayed
They've waved goodbye
They've wiped an eye
They've fished a brook
They've held a book
These hands are wrinkled now, and old
With all the years they worked to mold
The things they thought that they should do
And all of it was just for you

THANK YOU GOD

Restful moments close my days
And fill my thoughts with thankful praise
For all the things God does for me, in many ways
And I am full of sorrow for the words I cannot find
To thank him for the blessings, in my heart and mind
I think He sees my lack of prose
The love for Him that fills my heart, I think He knows

SILENT WAIT

My days are filled with silent wait
My nights with agony
In hurt I wear a scarlet cloak
For all the world to see
And all the loveless minutes float
Like flotsam to the shore
And dissipate in dying waves
And then they are no more
And I cannot release them
With no power to command
My love lays shipwrecked on the shore
All broken on the sand
How better to have known it not
Nor sailed life's bitter sea
Then have these days of silent wait
And nights of agony

THE DAWN

In the dead hours of morning
When it's neither night nor day
And we are truly all alone
In thought and our own way
When we have no objectives
And dreams lay quiet, still
And visions shimmer to and fro
And we are weak of will
When our hearts beat loudly
And future beckons, pale and wan
The timid souls reluctant rise
To face with fear another dawn

TIME TO BE

Life for some, a day
And then it goes away
But quality of time
One really can't define
Each precious hour sent
And cherished as it went
The wasted time and days
We lose along the ways
Are gathered up in years
And tied with pain and tears
And we never even see
How precious these could be
For it's only with regret
We see time we have, and yet
We waste still more, and say
There'll be another day

GOD TAKES MY HAND

Behind my heart where all my broken dreams are kept
And all the words I cannot say
And all the tears I have not wept
God sees it all and knows me deep
He stirs my weary aching heart
And wakens all the dreams that sleep
And takes my hand and leads me on
To my tomorrow

I'LL LEAVE MY HEART

Sea, sand, and seagulls
Gladden my heart
Diamonds on sea waves
Make it hard to depart
To the world that is calling
And the things I must do
A picture of duty
Replaces this view
Sea, sand, and seagulls
Make it hard to depart
I'll go, for I must
But I'll leave my heart

WHAT AM I?

Happiness sits just outside my vision
In shadows, like tomorrow
I cannot call the new day forth
It does not fit my sorrow
As if they both have their place
And shapes and shades of color
Laced and woven in my days
White hot to faded grey, and duller
Until the new time comes, and I may wear
The elusive coat of happy days
That lingers tantalizing near
But I am armed with memories
And know those days are only lent
For tomorrow takes my joy away
And brings me discontent

If I could judge the weather of my feelings
If I could balance minutes, seconds, days
Perhaps the pendulum of my thoughts
Could make me feel serene always
But then I would be someone I don't know
I cannot visualize this other me
I wear the raiment of my thoughts
For everyone to see

ANOTHER PRECIOUS DAY

If I could live life over
There's lots of things I'd do
I'd think each thought more deeply
And feel them deeper too
I'd watch a lot more sunsets
And walk a lot more miles
And change more strangers into friends
With good talk, and more smiles
I'd spend my minutes wisely
And sift each word I say
And thank the Lord for giving me
Another precious day

FLOWERS OF HOPE

I walked in my garden, and saw growing there
The thorn bush of trouble, the weeds of despair
I tended them daily, with my discontent
And watered them often, with tears misery sent

I walked in God's garden, and found growing there
The flowers of hope, the bright blooms of care
The sunshine of smiles, the gladness of love
All watered with faith sent from heaven above

DREAMS

Dreams that never end, are unfulfilled
But still the dreamers dream each day
And the years pass and die
And dreams are scattered on the way

Not noticed be the dreaming one
Their path is warm and straight ahead
They do not see with passing time
That some are worn, and some are dead

And at the end of life and time
I would hope that they would see
Their battered dreams, as sweet and clear
And hold them close like me

REST

I have no doubt that heaven is more blessed
That all shines brighter, that laughter's lighter
Since Mother went to rest
And all that grows, like flowers, are more fair
That angels smile more often, with Mother living there
Sometimes down here on earth, I feel somehow
When I am lost, and cannot do my thing
She comes and puts her soft lips to my brow
And I can hear the herald angels sing

SOMETHING THAT I DIDN'T DO

What happened to your happy smile
I saw it yesterday
Is it something that I didn't do
That made it go away
Your eyes held stars and twinkled
But now are dull and flat
Is it something that I didn't do
That makes them look like that
Your spirit I admired
You bubbled when we met
Is it something that I didn't do
Some hurting, or neglect
It was never my intention
To change you into sad
I loved you, just the way you were
I knew just what I had
So bring me back that happy smile
That I saw yesterday
Tell me what you need of me
To make sad go away

JUST FOR AWHILE

Feet that never ran upon the sand
Or felt the crunch of dry leaves in the fall
A little face that never felt the sun
He was so new, there wasn't time at all
He never saw the pictures in a book

Nor learned the printed words that lay beneath
No wonderland to fill his little mind
No childish game of hide and seek
And like a breath of spring, he came
An angel sent to brighten so few days
And nothing left to fill my hungry heart
But memories soft soft haze

LEARNING OF GOODNESS

I didn't hardly know the Lord, when I was just a lad
I hadn't grown, I hadn't learned, and I was awful bad
For there was lots of tempting things to sway a little kid
So I indulged myself in all, in everything I did
And the devil laughed, and held my hand; and followed me each day
He fought the good that was in me and kept the Lord at bay
And as the years flew by so fast, I heard voice inside
Say, "His promises will not be kept." It said, "The devil lied."
And I, with little wisdom, could see a far off light
It shone so beautiful and warm, the golden rays of right
I reached my hand; it was a start to peace, and hope, and prayer
To take me in, to take me home, for God is always there
And now though I am wanting, in lots I do and say
I have the knowledge of His love, that I can live His way
I speak of God to everyone, His love and life I share
And they in turn will understand that God is everywhere

I'LL GET BY

Worries and troubles I wish they had wings
Bad days, and nightmares, and horrible things
And the work just piles up higher each day
I have to see to it, I can't let it lay

I've even gained weight that I can't seem to fight
And I'm poured in my clothes, it's a comical sight
I live on a budget, there's things that I lack
Some women are thrifty, I don't have the knack

Would you say I'm discouraged, heavens, not me
For a positive outlook to life, is the key
Oh well, said I to myself, with a sigh
I lift up my chin; wipe a tear from my eye

There's no use complaining, or making a fuss
My boat has just sailed, and I've missed the bus
But as long as I'm breathing, I just shake my head
If I pinch and it hurts, then I know I'm not dead

THE CALL

When no one needs me anymore
I'll say my prayers and close the door
And walk within the forest green
And feel as if I've never been
When no one wants me anymore
The memories of days of yore
Will lose their glow to keep me warm
And all is gone both face and form
For life that well worn trodden path
The winds of time, its cruel wrath
Will blow the years, and time away
And I am left with just today
There are no feelings left at all
As I await the far off call
I hear the song, it's getting late
And I in turn, sing back, I WAIT

BE CAREFUL

I cried last night enough to fill a bucket
The night before enough to sail two ships
My body has been helpless, and it seems no one could care less
And I'm the holder of two unkissed lips
My feet have stopping their tapping to life's music
My heart no longer beats to nature's rhyme
My eyes stare at the clock, as I listen to it tock
When the phone rings, I jump higher every time
And this waiting sure plays havoc with a body
I can't eat, my food lays dried up on my plate
And they say I'm getting thinner, when I do not eat my dinner
I'm bound to end up in a sorry state
But this is just the same old love story
The kind you hear them singing everyday
About the guy that took it all and went away
Do you think maybe, that I have learned a lesson
And will I guard my heart, and be so wise
When a new love comes along, will I listen to its song
And be engulfed again until it dies
Oh listen to my story, every Mary, Jane, and Kate
Be oh so very cautious when you go out on a date
Eat, drink, and make merry, where ever you may roam
Take your table manners with you, but leave your heart at home

THE WRITERS

It's funny that we do not hear
About the man who writes in rhyme
The things he saw, and felt, and lived
About another place and time
Though many never know his name
Obscure he lives, obscure he dies
His spirit is on every page
We hear his laugh, we hear his cries
And I can feel such empathy
As if he were here at my side
We hear his heart and know him well
Within the sunset he describes
And there are books of prose and verse
With signatures, I do not know
I read the lines, and feel the thoughts
Of Shelly, Shakespeare, Burns, and Poe
Is it enough for poet's past
To fill the page with thought and rhyme
And feel content to see them thus
And leave them for another time
And hope that they may touch a heart
Relive the words, and feel the dream
That sets the spirit far apart
I say that it's enough for me
If I fulfill their destiny

THE LIGHT

If just a tiny little light
Will help us make it through
Like a beacon in the future
That we can struggle to
As if a strong hand holds us
And guides us from the past
To a better day tomorrow
In a shadow it will cast
For the corners that are dark with gloom
Are dreaded by us all
The grey sharp memories that haunt
The blackness we recall
Can only be dispelled for good
By looking to the light
And having hope, and having faith
And fighting the good fight

HIDDEN TRUTHS

Truth is only in the heart, for no one is so brave
To speak it out, both loud and clear, but takes it to the grave

For if it were to be thus shared, and not received in kind
The gold of truth would tarnish, so it is kept in mind

To find a kindred soul in truth, is very rare indeed
The light of truth, to all, will find a shining need

But we wear our pride, and hold it close, and we can do no less
Encumbered by its burdens, that we should lay to rest

And pride holds truth so quiet, it's never brought to view
But trembles there within the heart, till life is through

POOR LITTLE PANSY

Poor little pitiful pansy
Prettily primping with pain
Your little elf's face turned up to the sky
Searching for one drop of rain

Planted in clumps by the window
Planted along by the ledge
And your flat, once green leaves
All withered and brown, are beginning to curl at the edge

Your face holds a puzzled expression
Your friend's a puzzled frown
While others, head bent, resigned to their fate
Just stare at the hard crusted ground

The sun does not care, and won't shade his glare
And man has forgotten your beauty
You were planted with care, and left sitting there
And the clouds have forgotten their duty

THE GOOD OLD DAYS

Those were the good old days they say
Their memories playing tricks
They remember all those days and years
But they get those memories mixed
They remember growing all of their food
They'd plant and reap and hunt
And sitting before a roaring fire
All toasty warm… in front
They forget the candles, and coal oil lamps
And ice cold beds at night
And wells, and outside privies
With both of them froze tight
How the milk stayed warm in the summer
If there wasn't ice in the chest
They remember all the good things
But forgetting all the rest
But maybe it doesn't matter
If it makes them happy to see
The picture of a rosy past
They hold in their memory
If it comforts them when they're tired and worn
And brings a smile to their face
There's hope and joy in memory
We can't see this a waste
For we all need something to help us go on
And the past can help us a lot
If it helps to remember the good old days
Why not?

REACHING

I cannot write a line today
I cannot find a word to say
I am full of turmoil, then
I cannot write the words today
All still upon the heart, they lay
Even though I want to share
Feelings lay in darkness there
But when I have a change of heart
I know the words and feelings start
And even if the time gets worse
I know that I will write a verse
For only from the high and low
Only from the joy and woe
Emotions feed my pen and so
From this the word and rhyme will flow
It may not shake the world, you see
But still it is a part of me

A COTTAGE SMALL

All I want is a cottage small
Along a quiet lane
And maybe an apple tree
And a wild rose vine to train
All I want in the cottage small
Is a soft and comfy chair
And at night a fire bright
And someone I love to share
All I want by the cottage small
Is a little lively brook
And on a hill some daffodil
Where my eyes and heart can look
In my cottage small at twilight time
I will fold up my worries and cares
And tuck them away till another day
For no pain will visit here

SECOND TIME

Have I been here before?
I am filled with longing, for days I never knew
A past before my time
Of quiet reverence and life in which I never grew
Of love spoken many times, of books and fires bright
So foreign to these days I live
But only they feel right
How am I placed in time so wrong, a feeling insecure?
The me I know, walked other paths
Through portals of another door
And only then do I feel still, for I am home
This time I feel so real, this dream
Wherein the spirits roam
But I will leave this place, this time
And journey to reality
Where I am but a faded print
Of what I'm meant to be

A MAGIC DAY

I have a reason to wake with the dawn
To open my eyes, to stifle a yawn
To look to the day, all rosy and new
The garden a promise all covered with dew
This is the time to think and to plan
To use every minute the best that I can
For the sun is a gift and it's given to me
From the dawn as it rose, till it sinks in the sea
Within that time as it shares its warm glow
I live, love, and feel more things, till I know
As I gather together a bouquet of thoughts
And feelings, and dreams, this new day has brought
Till the minutes are spent, like a magical wand
And I say goodnight, as the sea claims the dawn

THE BALM OF TIME

There is no real world here today
I arose and worked to gain the wealth
Performed my duties word and deed
But all the time I never felt

I couldn't tell if it was fair
I couldn't say with what I dealt
The shadows fell and passed away
But all the time I never felt

I didn't feel a spring in heart
I didn't see the sky above
No flowers grew along my path
I didn't see or speak of love

An emptiness for all the while
There was that missing something sweet
An urgent call a distant note
That I must hurry up and meet

We cannot change our mood by rote
We cannot force a feeling fair
Pretend that all our minutes count
If that feeling is not there

We each of us must walk our path
And let the hours seek to heal
And count our blessings, every one
And suddenly we feel

THE WATCHER

No doubt there are folks, out there so they say
That do their own thing that go their own way
And don't seem to care what tomorrow may bring
But live for today, and do their own thing
But me, how I ponder on worldly affairs
My heart full of sorrow, my head full of cares
I feel I should do a lot more every day
But to venture forth boldly, just isn't my way
For I am just one, and the little I do
Just seems to solve nothing, things come back anew

Each day full of problems is all that I see
And they'll never be solved if it's left up to me
The future is fraught with peril and plight
And it needs an army, to fight the good fight
But my armchair is comfy, and so I dream on
And life uses me, in its game as a pawn
And so I am programmed and changed every day
And watch other folks just go their own way

A WALK ALONE

Although I bend down on my knees
I find it hard to pray
There's lots I want to tell the Lord
But cannot find the words to say

But if I take a walk alone
Among the things that God creates
I seem to rid myself a bit
Of earthly greed, of fear and hate

And somehow though He does not speak
The wonders of His world indeed
Impart to me the peace and calm
The faith and hope I sorely need

And though another day will come
When I'll be back to court despair
I'll take my walk alone again
And find that God's still waiting there

THE BABY YEARS

I saw an angel yesterday
And she was meant for me
I knew that she was coming
All pink and sweet and cuddly

But oh I never thought that she
Would own me from the start
Entwine her little life with mine
Her fingers round my heart

And as the days moved into years
And we grew far apart
My memory sees her baby face
And feel her fingers round my heart

ALL ALONE

I will not stay alone and grieve
To see the flowers die again
Or hear the soft wind whisper
A long forgotten name

There is no pleasure to my eye
And all the things that I held dear
The faces that can tear my heart
Are now just objects mounted here

The clocks are ghosts that tic and run
And time gives heartache, no relief
And moonlight does not show the way
To give away my grief

REPEAT

Time absorbs each day, each thought
Each word we do not say
And all the feelings deep inside
In time just fade away
And all our good intentions
And good deeds never met
Just lay upon the passing days
And leaves us with regret

A heart that should be full of love
Is crowded now with pain
For all the things we should have done
Come back to haunt again
And the bitter words in anger
We wish we could delete
Are pressed on hearts each day of time
Their pain repeat

THE MOON

High in the sky so round so white
The moon will stand, a prince, a knight
To watch the lovers making plans
To see them kiss and holding hands
He knows the mettle of their fire
He sees ahead what will transpire
But does not censure, does not say
But watches as the lovers play
Sometimes he almost disappears
And does not see the lover's tears
He slips behind a floating cloud
As lovers often cry aloud
He's seen the works of love before
And cannot stand it anymore
Because he knows that love will die
No matter how the lovers try
He knows that there are very few
Who keep their love all bright and new
Who work at loving everyday
With what they do, and what they say
He knows that love is for the living
It does not take, but ever giving
High in the sky so round so white
The moon will smile on these tonight
And watch these lovers with moon pride
And send his silver light to guide

THE REAL REALITY

I used to think that when I die
There would be grief and fear
But now that I am growing old
And feel death ever near

It seems to me like gentle sleep
With someone waiting by
And all my loved ones I have missed
Surrounding where I lie

They take my hand just like a babe
Because it's new to me
And all my burdens, now I will leave
I'm resting finally

I hope that this is not a dream
That when I die I'll see
That this new life will be the start
Of real reality

SWEET LAUGHTER

Nobody noticed her while she was here
And nobody noticed her now fading hair
She fetched and she carried as she had before
And nobody spoke as they passed by her door

They took her for granted and down through the years
No one held her hand, no one saw her tears
And her voice was a whisper as years took their toll
And she thought it's to be, when you're finally old

But inside was a girl, with feelings laid bare
Inside was a girl without toil or care
And her voice held sweet laughter, her voice held a song
It never knew anger or fury or wrong

And God saw her sweetness, and God saw her worth
All of the days she spent here on earth

JUST FEELING

Don't ask me who I am, for I don't know
I lean to left or right, whichever way the wind will blow
My thoughts and dreams are scattered on the breeze
My heart and feelings scarred, by wearing them upon my sleeve

And if you ask me why, I could not say
I wrestle with each minute, and each day
As if my eyes are closed to all the world
I fly no flag, and miss the gauntlet hurled

I have not come to grips with second chance
I would not recognized it at a glance
But move ahead, because I dare not stand
For all to see my tears, and outstretched hand

The past has placed me here, could I but see
The time I drifted to this place, this me
There is a longing for a past, not clear
Some soft blurred sweetness off somewhere

And when this day, this time, comes stealing
I am nothing, except feeling

FAULTY MCBAIN

Faulty McBain was a sailor
He fought for the land of the free
Until they sent him back to the shore
For falling five times in the sea
And this was the life of Faulty McBain
Day after day it was so
If anyone spoke to him, it was to ask
A question that he didn't know
When he ate certain foods he'd break out in a rash
And people avoided him then
His hair wouldn't lay, and he'd sneeze in the hay
And this had been since he was ten
But Faulty McBain had a dream just the same
Someday he'd be well liked, and rich
So he bought every lottery ticket he could
Thinking this may just do the trick
One day, to the surprise of all that he knew
His number was called from the wicket
But Faulty McBain's bad luck would hold
He couldn't find the ticket

THE LOST DOLL

Why the tears my little friend?
Why that sad small face?
Little paths among the grime
Where tears have left their trace
Why are you sad and lonely
On such a lovely day
You had your doll just a moment ago
And now she's gone away

Well dolls don't just get up and walk
Oh! I'm sorry, I didn't know
That your little doll could cry and crawl
And even her hair could grow
And her eyes can sleep, and she can speak
And her dress is made of silk
And surely by now, she needs a change
For she can drink real milk

This little mother was worried
And fear had filled her eyes
And as she called her dolly dear
She'd listen for dolly cries
But the world was a dark and silent place
As we walked there hand in hand
And the searchers joined, and added on
To the ever growing band

But the dark eyed, dark haired dolly
Was nowhere to be found
As we searched through the lonely forest
And didn't hear a sound
The night hawk and the blue jay
Searched in the upper trees
Looking in nests and thickets
Searching all of these

The rabbit hopped through the holly hedge
And the fox over every mound
The squirrel and chipmunk followed along
But the dolly couldn't be found
"What if it should rain," said a dog
Who happened to run by
Unless she's under a mushroom
The little girl started to cry

But suddenly, "Mama" said a voice from the dark
Mama was repeated again
They all heard the voice distinctly
As they hurried down the lane
And the face of her doll reflected
In the lights from the distant farm
And the little mother held her
And the searchers cried, "Hurrah!"

And they all felt thankful and happy
What a perfect end to the day

REGRETS

A little bit of this and that, a little bit of tit for tat
And arguments are born
A little bit of push and shove, a little bit of hate, no love
And hearts are torn
In time we find we rue the day, in time we find the words we say
Lay bitter in our hearts
For all the words we say so free, lay back upon our memory
We've forgotten how it starts
Maybe within a week, a year, maybe the pain is less to bear
But so hard to forget
In retrospect this needn't be, in retrospect we now can see
It leaves us with regret

TWAS THE WEEK BEFORE CHRISTMAS

Twas the week before Christmas
And all through the house
I've scrubbed, waxed, and polished
To make things look nice
To have it all shiny for Santa to see
I've garlanded, and lighted, and trimmed up the tree
The parcels are wrapped with surprises inside
Secured from the places that they had to hide
The fire is layed, and the baking is done
With a bell on the door to greet everyone
So now I am waiting for folks I love best
Who arrive rosy cheeked, to fill up my nest
There's greeting to friends, that live far away
My thoughts are of you, on this Christmas day
There is nothing better, than hearing from you
In a long friendly letter, to tell me what's new
For Santa could leave me pure gold, and I'd say
It would rival your letter, on this special day

THOUGHTS

High on the hill I see the world
I paint the scene with tears of joy
And frame it with the thoughts of love
And hang it on my memory
And only God and I can see

High on the hill is there for all
Who look for good, and heed its call
Upon the hill a scene sublime
If one allows their thoughts to climb

THE PASSAGE OF TIME

A man's worth is measured by what he is capable of doing
What he has learned through the passage of time
And how he applies this knowledge in the time left to him
Having gained wisdom through experience
Sifting out the worthwhile and filing the useless
If only to serve as a bad example
A person growing will count his mistakes as stepping stones to maturity
See man in his true light, look for the tiny bit of goodness in all
Accept life as the imperfect holiday it is,
Death, the gate at the end of life's walk
And living, the preparation to enable us to walk through gracefully

TIME

While we are waiting we must live
Spend the passing time, or ignore it, either way it will go
The end is only seen by those that choose to look to the future
Others do not think, or if they do, fear takes their moments
And makes of them something other then they could be
But we all meet at the same place
Filled with satisfaction or regret, rendering a lifetime
Into nothingness…

CHANGES

And when in time each sun is set
We do not feel a dull regret

For things we have not said or done
Before the setting of the sun

So now we view the fading past
With bitterness, in memory last

It's our own years, we each arrange
And all of these we cannot change

THE GOLDEN DOOR

Go and fetch her, bring her to me
She has wearied oh so long
In life's battles she had courage
In her living she was strong

Did God's bidding helping others
As she struggled with each day
Only asking help from Jesus
As she bent her head to pray

And she never asked of Jesus
Anything just for herself
Just for others did she seek Him
Just for others pray for help

And the angels took her gently
Brought her through that golden door
Up to sit in Jesus' glory
Where life's worries are no more

THE SOUL

The soul is the essence of life
The factory for laughter and tears
The producer of all of the good things of life
Down through the billions of years

It's the well of love, the holder of birth
Where the dreams of all good men begin
The sole container of all human worth
Devoid of original sin

THE FALL

I see the autumn leaves are turning at the tip
So tired they are sailing down, because they lost their grip

And spread upon the ground, a carpet red and gold
I don't see why they're tired, they're just one season old

And the flowers, it seems like yesterday I saw them there
Now all withered up and brown, they soon will disappear

And God will spread a blanket, to keep them day and night
A blanket, oh so soft and warm, a mantle of pure white

And we can walk right on them, and they will feel no pain
They sleep a sleep that's undisturbed until its spring again

MEMORIES OF DEAD LOVES

Love, like dead leaves, lay on the frozen ground
Curled and twisted tortured shapes
Blown by the winds of time, around
So sad, once jubilant in youth

The future summer still ahead
With all romantic dreams to spin
They now lay close to dead
And soon they will be gone

But not forgotten I will say
Dead loves are tucked in someone's heart
The winds of time can't blow away

SOFT ARMS

I have no coat of precious fur
Or car of gleaming chrome
Or yacht, or money in the bank
Or mansion for a home
But I have arms so soft so white
That wrap around, and hold me tight
And make me feel the world is right
Because I am a mother

LOVE REACHED OUT

Love reached out to touch me
But I wasn't there
It hung suspended in the soft spring air
Love smiled at me in passing
And I wondered why
Not knowing what I missed
I didn't even cry

FIRST LOVE

A first love never leaves you
No matter what the time

A first love seems to linger
To tease and taunt the mind

And as the years are played out
With every twist and turn

A first love stays in memory
To make you yearn

JUST A GLIMPSE

Just a glimpse of a spirit
Dancing by
Just a glimpse of a spirit
From the corner of my eye
Of course I'm told this could not be
They would not show themselves to me
I think they do it just to tease
Because they know, that I am pleased

SPRING WILL COME

In my garden in the fall, I harvest all, and can
I marmalade, I jelly, I relish, and I jam
And after all is put away, I close my winter door
Until the day I hear the spring, and winter is no more

Again all nature wakens, and I in turn the same
I plant my future flowers; I know them all by name
And watch the evenings linger, and feel the sun's warm ray
I see a new beginning, I live it everyday

But oh too soon it's ended, for winter will not stay
Her wrath on flower, bush, and tree
Now spring is only here again in memories

LONGING FOR SPRING

When everything is brown and dead
It makes me long to see the spring
Where dusty lanes my feet may tread
To see the blue bird on the wing
Inching back into my mind
The winter sun warms memories
Of daffodils and daisy chains
And old rope swings on maple trees

THE CANARY

He sits within his cage and sings
On his perch, with useless wings

Beneath is gravel, water, seed
He is lucky, yes indeed

Sometimes he doesn't even tweet
Or keep his feathers clean and neat

But watches birds out in a tree
And thinks, I wish that it was me

THE BABIES GRAVE

There was a man his hair was white
His name I knew it not, and yet
His face a mask, his shoulders bent
He is a man I'll not forget

My baby sweet, so small and sweet
He made a bed up for my babe
Through the years I see him yet
This man that dug my baby's grave

THE FEELING TIMES

I do not mind the sad times, when tears may fall
I do not mind a lump in throat, when memories I recall

Nor do I mind a happy laugh, a joyful day
Euphoric times as long as they may stay

I cannot cope, or figure out the in between
With neither joy or sorrow, and nothing felt or seen

The minutes like long hours, each day will last
The feeling times, a step away, just from my grasp

And I am not alone, in limbo state
But hold the hands of all, who like me wait

TIME TO PRAY

Oh tell me the right time to pray Lord
Oh tell me the hour and day
And tell me where best to kneel Lord
And give me a hint what to say

And understand when I've been bad Lord
A mere mortal is all that I am
So help me today, and show me the way
And I'll do the best that I can

THE SILENT HILLS

The silent hills their century stands
As Mother Nature takes a hand
To heal the scars of passing man
No monolithic come to view
But bleached white roots, that nature slew

As laughing waters seem to say
We watched the mortals at their play

LOOKING BACK

Each minute that I wait for happiness
Lie long upon my days
And time seems to stretch so far
Along the weary ways
The path I tread is strange to me
And not my own
Unfamiliar and bleak, I tread each step
And all alone
But somehow I cannot turn back
For I have spent a lifetime on these ways
Practice steps not always what we choose
Worn paths in memory, we follow all our days
Sometimes we find they do not fit us snug
But chafe and bring a weary tear
We must accept our lot in life
This a cross, that we must bear

THE GRAVEYARD

My footsteps were drawn
Where the grey marble grew
Where the flowers lay fair
O'er the folks that I knew

Where the quietness robbed
The birds of their song
And memories shadows
Lay deep and long

JUST TODAY

I cannot see tomorrow, for all my yesterdays
They fill my eye, and crowd my mind
And work their subtle ways
As time comes softly stealing
And steals my years away
And takes my dreams to some far place
And leaves me just today

DEAR TO ME

I hear your sweet voice calling
I feel you ever near
I see your white head nodding
I see your face so dear

It's just as if you never left
You are so dear to me
Your goodness and your loving warmth
Remain in memory

MISTY MOUNTAINS

Morning
I wake to misty mountains, outside my window sill
I wake with heart so full of hope, when everything is still
I wake with expectations, the grass still wet with dew
But when the day is over, the mountains turn gold
The sun has set, and now the earth, is tinted black and cold

But I know that in the morning, nature made me so aware
If I search the misty mountains, all that beauty will be there

A BEE VIEW

I saw a little buttercup all by it's self alone
Except a bee sat on the edge
Like on a golden throne
He came to gather pollen
This is his life, his fate
Then lumbered to the edge, and flew
And thus did abdicate

MY PAST

What am I doing here and now?
When with a backward glance I see
A time and place, and just a thought
Can beckon and I long to be

Maybe nostalgia's all it is
That wistful print of memory
But why my heart will jump with joy
With every thought that comes to me

Because the future is not seen
The present does not please the mind
We seek to live our yesterdays
By holding close the tie that binds

But in truth by going back
To search the dreams we threw away
We will not find our future hopes
In some forgotten yesterday

Today, we shape the years ahead
And we must put the past aside
The tempting times, familiar thoughts
For going back will tantalize

But I could sit and dream all day
The future holds no memory
The past is sweet, and holds me close
And beckons and I long to be

THE USERS

If I was as free as a bird said I
As I watched them fly on wing
If I was as free as a bird I sighed
I'd not ask for another thing

But then as I saw them fly en mass
I wondered just who would stalk
The happy flight of those lovely birds
And then I saw the hawk

I lay in a field of golden grain
And envied them reaching high
I fingered each sun drenched golden stem
And then I saw the scythe

I saw my love and my heart grew full
I loved him more each day
And nothing could shatter my happiness
But my love was taken away

Our minutes are numbered, so hold them close
And our days grow fewer with time
We are users, not owners and just passing through
And nothing is yours or mine

FATHER TIME

Each wrinkle tells each year I've spent
The pain and worries, each event
And happiness does not for me
Turn back the years, as you can see

We all grow older every day
No matter what we do we pay
With wrinkles, fat, and silver hair
The mirrors show are always there

We exercise and cream our face
And every day it is a race
To turn back clocks with passing time
But finally we pass our prime

So you and I, must now agree
That this is as it's meant to be
And disregard youths fading call
And turn the mirrors to the wall

SISTER DEAR
Dedicated to my sister who passed away with Alzheimer's

I look at you, but do not see
The sparkle in your eye
You look at me, but vaguely
And do not see the tie
I see you as you were to me
And I remember when
We were so close, and we would talk
I'd like that time again
You left upon a journey
To somewhere I don't know
You left me here all by myself
I wish that I could go
Then hand in hand we'd wander
Down lanes we never knew
Is there adventure where you go
And magic things to do
And do you dream, like as a child
When you are all alone
And live it our in daily works
That others don't condone
Each day you travel farther
There's nothing left of old
And when I hold your hand in mine
It's cold

A GARDEN WALK

I walked my garden path and saw
A whole new world for me
As bluebells rang and daisies danced
And all in harmony

The path led to a little brook
With water clear and free
And on and on, until I saw
Beneath a willow tree

A grassy spot of velvet green
To sit and rest awhile
The whisper of the merry brook
That sang a merry mile

And I was filled with feelings
I cannot put to words
But nature told my story
In the singing of the birds

EVERYTHING I NEED

God's nearer in my garden
For all that He made grow
Is by His tender blessings
Not one thing did I sow

I sit and watch the wonders
And drink in all I see
And marvel at the gifts
That He bestowed on me

I hear the tiny sparrow
I know He sees it fall
And everything that lives is His
He hears the robin call

God's nearer in my garden
In tranquil time and space
My world is rose and violet
My world is filled with grace

DAWN SHADOWS

Dawn shadows on the forest grass
Paint tree and bush a different hue
Now rising over morn cloud fast
Another day all bright and new
Dawn shadows on the morning grass
Moving with the morning sun
Ascending to the tree tops fast
And now they're gone

MORNING HILLS

Peeking through the morning mist
Are morning hills
Their color is a different hue
A clash of wills
That do not measure up in memory
To those I knew
The mists that lay and separate
A changing view
Tomorrow on a clear morn
It will be
A different scene, a changing scene
That puzzles me
And when it rains.....

TRAVEL

I travel without moving
I just sit in my easy chair
And I can see and feel it all
Even though I am not there

You say it's not the same
A substitute, so it may seem
But I enjoy my travels
Every time I sit and dream

MEMORIES

No matter how the years will go
Teddy bears and dolls you'll find
Thinking back to yesterday
Those thoughts will bring them back to mind

And how the years will fall away
And each of us a child once more
Will see and feel that time again
With just a push on memories door

It is sometimes with aching heart
That we can touch that other day
And hold so close those teddy bears
And lay our grown up cares away

And suddenly we are again
That small and gentle child so pure
That holds true love, and is content
With just a push on memories door

GO BACK TO THE GARDEN

Let's go back to the garden
With roses and baby lace
And stay till the twilight deepens
And the stars fall on our face
Where quiet is long and lasting
No untrue word is said
But the sweet sound of whispered prayers
As we bow our weary head

Let's sit beneath the willow tree
Away from the eyes of man
And think of the joys of tomorrow
As everybody can
If they believe in God
Have faith in each new day
We may live a life of hope, and
Go back to the garden to stay

TIME

I searched my days, I searched my heart
Way back where shadows lay
The nameless years have stolen all
The long forgotten days

And there was only dry and brown
Like flowers when they die
These imprints of a memory
Quiet as a sigh

And I have lost all I have been
I did not even know
This faded shadow of myself
This weariness, and so

I stare ahead and close my eyes
For fear I would lose track
Of aimless wanderings and thoughts
No courage to look back

So they remain behind me
These promises and lies
I see them only dimly
Through old and tear filled eyes

But if I had the courage
And I could shed this pride
I'd be the child I used to be
I cannot for I've tried

Thus time is now my nemesis
Unforgiving, stark and cold
It took my dreams, it took my youth
And left me old

BOX OF GOLD

In a little box of gold
I secretly have hid
Is love, warm love just laying there
Until I lift the lid

And there it stayed all shiny new
Like gold and silver bright
Then flowed out like a river
To flood the day and night

And nothing here can stop it
It is so magical
And you can have as much of it
Until your heart is full

It will not lose its brilliance
As its treasures you unfold
To warm your heart and bless your days
Until you're very old

And when you're just a memory
In someone's heart to hold
This love is kept for someone else
In a little box of gold

TREASURES

I look to the stars for my diamonds
And I couldn't ask for more
They shine and glitter much brighter
Than those in the jewellery store

And the birds song in the forest
Is glorious, I must admit
More thrilling and sweet, and a much better treat
Than the band in the orchestra's pit

And the soothing roll of the ocean
That lulls me to sleep with its song
Each wave murmurs sweet, as it rolls to my feet
And the echoes, in memory last long

So why would I ask for anything more
Or wait for tomorrow to bring
Other treasures to show, for surely I know
Today I have everything

MY WINTER TIME

I remember back to spring
The yesterdays of long ago
With childish thoughts, and childish games
That left me with their afterglow

But faded into summer time
When living was no game at all
The sharpness of each passing day
With hurt and pain, I now recall

And as I changed from tenderness
To wary traveller in time
Each thought and deed was strange to me
I did not know them then as mine

But as the summer days depart
The autumn days my thoughts confine
And I am gentle once again
And softly live my winter time

I'D LIKE TO CALL BACK SUMMER TIME

I'd like to call back summer time
When things were warm and bright
My world was full of flowers
They made me feel all right

Somehow it chased away the fear
That crept into my heart
In times of cold and winter
In times of quiet dark

And though I searched my heart for pain
It slipped between my dreams of thought
The sunlight filled my searching eyes
Like dew, upon a web is caught

And I saw only happiness
And all the flowers fair
And heard the birds with sweet sweet song
They sang away my care

THE CHANGE

The music in my soul is gone
My heart no longer sings
And all the beauty flies
As if my days had wings

To some place dark and lonely
To lay alone and bare
Forgotten in the stillness
Without a thought or care

And time spins out unknowingly
The days of my neglect
I hold the hand of darkness
And dwell upon regret

A brand new day is coming
Is it too late to start
To follow sunny paths of mind
With just a change of heart

THE PAIN

Pain that does not leave with tears
But takes its place in every day
In all the mundane things I do
And will not go away

Beneath the laughter it's still there
And hidden in a smile
And though you do not see it
I feel it all the while

For I remember yesterday
A faded picture blurred and grey
Of happy times with happy thoughts
A second and they drift away

And I am filled once more with pain
It's laced within each minute spent
And in my dreams, it's ever close
Grips each and every hour sent

I do not see tomorrow clear
For time has blended night and day
And sight and touch is all the same
And passes quickly to decay

There is no joy in what I do
Or facing yet these weary years
I cry because I have the pain
This pain that does not leave with tears

THE STAGE OF LIFE

Another day is dawning
And I can see that I
With measured steps, that happiness
Again, will pass me by
As I begin performing
I listen to the clock
As I am led by retrospect
With every tick and tock
I see myself accepting
Life's chant every day
I follow every line and cue
Like acting in a play
The script proclaiming destiny
And I must play my part
I do not change or deviate
I know each day by heart
My actions are thus marked precise
No change without just cause
Until the final curtain, and
The whisper of an angel's wings
Is my applause

WHAT IF?

If we didn't have a memory
We'd be an empty shell
With nothing there to think about
And nothing there to tell
A sunset would not linger
A flower fill our eye
We would not ponder on this earth
With thoughts, and questions why
A friendship would be fleeting
A song would not be sung
A love would never touch the heart
And tears would not be wrung
Each day would be pattern
Of the day that went before
And we'd all be automated
Ever more

SILVER GREY

They just believe in black and white
There are no shades of grey
And everything is thought about
And planned for every day

And time must happen as its thought
No room for dreams or change
It would disturb the black and white
The pessimist, arranged

And those that do not thus conform
Who see the silver grey
Are thought as odd, one of a kind
Who follow their own way

And though the dreamers see the right
Of everyone's desire
Are looked upon as foolish men
For the dreams that they acquire

And those that do not look ahead
Or learn from past mistakes
Will see the visionary's dreams
A prelude to heart break

And though they may be always right
In the hindsight that they see
A dreamer dares to change it all
For the visions that might be

For dreamers do not waste their time
In worries and in doubt
Or listen to the black and white
But do what they're about

And even lend a helping hand
To dreamless souls that stray
And let them share the wonders of
Their days of silver grey

ARTIFICIAL WORLD

I'm not afraid of dying
But I fear from day to day
In this artificial world
That the real will slip away

I live an artificial life
In an artificial flat
I have an artificial dog
And an artificial cat

No flowers grow upon my sill
There is no room for that
You have artificial flowers
When you're living in a flat

The time goes by so quickly
And you do not think, or feel
And there's just one thought
Deep in my mind

If heaven will be real

ONE DAY AT A TIME

Around the bend on an unknown road
A secret waits to be found
Just ahead in the waning day
A lone loon's call will sound

A pleasant thought or just a smile
Or someone we've yet to meet
Fills the heart, with such a warm feeling
Like flowers beneath our feet

And when the silver stars will shine
And another day is spent
We may heave a sigh, with spirits high
And a feeling so content

MEMORIES TO HOLD

Thoughts of you caress my mind
And warm my heart and soul
New found friends to cherish
Some memories of old

But all are stopping posts in thought
And each a given sign
That march across my days and years
The markers of my time

And I would be a lonely soul
Without those golden days
To feel the goodness of a friend
Along the yearly ways

And as I share your thoughts and prayers
As you are sharing mine
We will walk life heart to heart
Until the end of time

THE SETTING SUN

Shadows on a country lane
Moving to the sun's refrain

With passing minutes of the day
They beckon now, and show the way

To travellers with quiet thought
And troubled souls, who often sought

A refuge, cool and quiet, green
Where not a living soul is seen

Maybe a place not too far
A running brook, a sandy bar

A log placed there to sit upon
To watching the dying of a dawn

I AWOKE

And as I watched, the day marched onward
More wonders did unfold
As nature showed me all her wares
And all her secrets told
And I in all my arrogance
Seemed now cut down to size
Compared to all of nature
It made me realize
I am merely passing through
Not pausing to reflect
The use I make of nature
Just my wanton and neglect
For what I deem as rightly mine
And use as I pass by
Is just the folding of a wing
The batting of an eye
And so all things will even out
For nature did intend
That we must pay, and measure up
Right at the end

AUTUMN

The angry waters argue with the shore
The blue bird and the robin are no more
The birch and willow form a leafless line
And nature says it is dying time

The spruce that danced a waltz, has lost its grace
And twirls and spins and loses all its lace
The gentle frost had formed upon each limb
As wild wind currents sing a stirring hymn

The cold wind from the northern waste
Comes now and tells all nature to make haste
His patience is short lived, his temper fine
He gives no second chance, these left behind

And you can feel stillness everywhere
As if the world kneels quietly in prayer
Expectant, breathless, beneath the winter's din
Nature waits with spring, another cycle to begin

A MOMENT IN TIME

I found a lovely spot today
With blues so blue, and greens so green
It took my breath away

Beneath this beauty lie
Daisies like white linen, and clouds so close
One wants to put their arms into the sky

And everything is sensuous
And all one heart can bear
It happened in a moment, standing there

SUN SET

I look to the west at the close of day
As the sun slips behind a hill
And I watch the colors that fuse the sky
As everything grows still

And the rosy glow turns to purple
And then to a midnight blue
And silhouettes the edge of my world
And the hills I thought I knew

And it filled my eye with beauty
And it filled my soul with song
The words lay quiet in my heart
But I hear them all night long

And memories bid me look again
To replenish my starving eye
And I watch till the night takes over
And lights each star in the sky

COURTING PAIN

I know that you are close
In physical form, but still
I cannot feel your loving warmth
And though I try, I never will

Why do I strive and yearn to touch
And practice my deceit
We seem to be a world apart
Only in my mind, is union sweet

But what is left of life, if I
Were suddenly to call a halt
And know my hopes for what they are
And lose loves battle by default

Then life to me would be a race
That I have run without a prize
The consequences I will face
Are pain and torment in disguise

For love is beauty, face and form
And does not show her sister strife
And we poor mortals, court them both
All our life

WISDOM

Happiness like a river runs through our lives
And like a desert the years run dry
And we know no reason why
And as man we take for granted
The lovely day the gentle night
And use them up as ever lasting
Never saving, never fasting
Now bewildered without answers
Like a child with hurt and tears
Our days to worry and to ponder
With the lean years left to wander
Foresight is a special blessing
Hindsight known to every man
Wisdom is our cane to hold on to, if we can

TOMORROW'S HOPE

Oh how I long for the days gone by
When each day I lived it seemed
The sun was warm on my upturned face
And filled my eyes with a dream

And the air was filled with perfume
From the flowers growing there
And you could touch my happiness
For it was everywhere

And each new day was special
Each second passing by
Held some new hope, to swell my heart
And make me question why

What fate decides my life to be
All hope and aspiration
What makes me wait tomorrow
With such wild anticipation

SPIRIT VOICES

In the woodland spirits dance
Bending grasses to and fro
And we say it's just a breeze
That's because we do not know
This other world of gnome and elf
We think the world is made up
Of people like ourselves
But in the woodland, in the moonlight
When the stars still wait on high
And the sunset spirits whisper
You can hear their plaintive cry
The world is then a place of wonder
Taking in the sun's last ray
Shaking off the worldly worries
You can feel them slip away
The spirits reach and blend around you
With arms of hope to give you peace
You are part of sky and forest
Pain and torment will release
I hear the world of distant voices
Calling, come, your place is here
The spirits say you still have choices
I hear their voices everywhere

WHAT WILL I DO

What will I do when all my dreams are dead
When all my hopes and thoughts put into words are said
When morn arrives all grey, and minutes lay
And the beauty in my eyes just fades away

And I cannot proceed a step, on naught
And left with nothing, but sadness brought
Despair a companion by my side
And seeks me out where ere I hide

I look with torchered thoughts, both day and night
Steeped deep in hurt and pain, I cannot put to right
And think upon the past until I ache
And live with all this pain until I wake

Except I see a flower there
God's calling cards, I tuck within my hair
A ray of sun that stirs a cold cold heart
And wakes the soul and makes the dreaming start

For only this, to thine own self be true
Quench your thirst with cool fresh morning dew
And see the world alone, all clean and sweet
Is all we need to live each day we meet

The doubting gone, the bright eye seeing clear
Ignore the shadows standing near
And live your dreams with hope and pride
For truth will have no need to hide

NEW LOVE

Deep in the heart there lays in wait
A love so good and pure
All soft in mystery and unused
To last forever more

A shining love within it's self
Beneath a halo bright
As like a shining silver star
That brightens up the night

A gift to give, awaits a love
To match it's own in winning
The other love, a matching love
And this is the beginning

THE PATH

My heart can reach the stars
But still I pine
The moon may light my way
But not be mine

I dream my dreams and wait
And waiting still
The minutes come and slip away
Far past tomorrow's hill

Like shadows all my hopes
Elude and stray as dreaming went
I stay the same and wait
But cannot be content

I reach again with heart
My thoughts I now condone
And know at last, through tears
We walk our paths alone

SADNESS

I live with sadness every day
It seems quite friendly in a way
It holds my hand, and shares my bed
It sometimes pushed, and sometimes led

And if by chance it slips my mind
Or if in memory left behind
I feel an emptiness inside
An emptiness I can't abide

For when I am alone you see
I'm lost to all I used to be
I feel the tears inside like wine
But do not know that they are mine

The tears I need just out of reach
The words I need in quiet speech
A friendly touch I seem to lack
To sort things out, to bring me back

And I must wait alone it seems
In hopeless state, without my dreams
Until warm sadness touches me
And wakes the feelings, lets me see

The past that I should lay away
The loves and dreams of yesterday
The bitter sweet beguiling ways
I keep beside me all my days

A CHRISTMAS CARD

It isn't that I do not think
About you through the year
And value all the memories
And thoughts that I hold dear

It's just when Christmas comes around
With candles all aglow
And carollers, and Christmas trees
I want to let you know

So have a merry Christmas
And I would like to say
That every day I think of you
It's a Christmas every day

LOVE'S MEMORY

I listen to the distant hills, I hear love's melody
It echoes from a dying past, and only meant for me
And as each note drops in my ear, it speaks a dreamy past
A song of hurts, a song of love, as echoing will last

I water violets with my tears; I hug the moss and pray
The agony and pain I feel, will only last a day
But time is long, and pain will hug, us ever close and teach
That what we need to still our pain, is ever out of reach

There are no words, there is no touch, to help a lover who
Loved not wisely, but too well, as all true lovers do
And at the end of life and time, we see in memory
These battered dreams as sweet and clear
And hold them close, like me

NEVER MISSED

All this beauty gone to waste
And never seen or hugged to heart
All life's music never sung
Just accepted as a part

Of all the moments that we use
With minutes days and years adorned
Just time that's passed
And never missed or mourned

OUR LIFE

My mind and heart will soar on high
A silver roadway far beyond
I travel light, like thistledown
The universe and I will bond
And I will know all things for now
And feel the pulse of life within
Absorbing all that ever was
Mankind and I become as kin
And all that's love is standing near
And sadness just a step away
And tears will well, for now I know
The mingled two I feel each day
Though I must come back to my place
And face tomorrow best I can
Armed with the knowledge I have learned
Not always shown to every man
For we must dream and contemplate
And hurt, and feel, and love, and give
And keep the pain close to our joy
This is our life to live

MY PRINCE

I listened to the old one
And what she said made sense
For she had age and wisdom
She had experience

She told me of the future
She said take heed and hear
Don't live your life a princess
There's lots of frogs out there

The things you read about romance
Aren't really true at all
You must be realistic
With the writing on the wall

I listened to her story
I thought about it since
But I know it was not meant for me
For I have met my prince

THE LONELY PRINCESS

This lonely room, with walls of pain
The days of hope are sought in vain
For death would be a haven sweet
This aching heart no longer beat
Or cling to life, with eyes to see
The future with its misery
But velvet soft, the starry night
To black the time, as soul takes flight
To fly as if on angel wings
And rest among unearthly things
For all this agony and more
Robbed me of all I had in store
Remove the sun, the moon, each star
My loss in more, yea more by far
And shame, for pride was taken too
And all the joy, when love was new
Unvalued when in giving best
The very soul, was worth far less
And though I long to have it end
I'm tied with strings that I attend
Life's weary duties, I am host
Though sadly, I am but a ghost

WHERE YOU ARE

There is a place it's not far
In all my dreams, that's where you are
Where golden sunlight never ends
And meadows green with paths that wend

And summer breeze is but a sigh
Birds sing all day, and flowers never die
When days are grey and full of pain
My hope is I'll see you again

There is a place it's not too far
In all my dreams that's where you are
And when I travel to that place
I'll hold you close and kiss your dear sweet face

ON HALLOWEEN

His crooked grin was all I saw
His leering smile, jaw to jaw

His shining skin, reflecting so
From eyes, to inner candle glow

The goblins, witches, ghostly things
That creep and crawl, and fly on wings

As little children shake with fright
And even though it lasts one night

Just once a year, is all he's seen
That once a year, is Halloween

The pumpkin

FINDING HEART

Most folks are just the same, I'd say
Finding heart to get them through yet another day
Performing every task, folks think they ought to do
And putting on a show, not really wanting to

Each day a repetition of the one that went before
And knowing that tomorrow has just the same in store
And the only thing that really helps, these folks to carry on
Is a picture of a dream that looms beyond

No man may know that dream, or how it may assist
To help them with their worries and sadness, they resist
You can call it hope or faith, or whatever you may please
But it will help, so help yourself to any of these

For we cannot travel far, if we travel all alone
And we need a helping hand, when we're facing the unknown
So most folks are just the same I'd say
Finding heart, or friend, to get them through yet another day

THE INNER VOICE

As I grow older I can see
The many faults I have in me
The selfishness in what I do
And that my virtues are so few
How could I spend that many days
In wanton times and cruel ways
Without a thought to what I did
Since I was just a little kid
I guess there may be some excuse
For childish acts, excess abuse

I didn't know the way I'd grow
In what direction I would go
It took a lot of living years
It took the joys, it took the fears
To teach me I could make a choice
To listen to that inner voice
And now the end is just in sight
I seem to do a few things right

A TIME

My joys in life are few
A fire bright, some stormy night
And thoughts of you
And when the lonesome time
Is more than I can bear
I look into the fire bright
And see you smiling there
And as the embers sing their song
Throw their shadows on the wall
That's when my joy lasts all night long

RARE MOMENT

I need a candle, and the quiet time
To hear only sounds of life
Like the laughter of a new dawn
And clear the memory of strife
To make this moment, seem real
To compare
And know in truth
This precious time so rare

REALITY

I have met the wicked witch
And ghouls in grungy clothes
I have walked on moonless nights
Been pounced upon by trolls

I have eaten wiggly worms
And drank from muddy brooks
I've been tripped and beaten on
And given dirty looks

But even so my head is high
And I may laugh out loud
While picking out my coffin
While trying on my shroud

For life is just a bumpy trip
We tread on weary feet
We pay for every step we take
And may not get a seat

Complaints will not avail us
A special place on earth
And virtue may side step us
Though we show our worth

So if you meet the wicked witch
Just smile don't make a sound
And you may meet someone who sits
At least that's what I've found

FILLED AGAIN

Was it a breeze, or an angel
That brushed my fevered brow
Is it hope that fills my aching heart
That's helping me right now
Peace that is sent at the close of day
In the twilight lasting long
And the voice of a guardian spirit
I hear in the robin's song
I feel that I am never alone
As I walk along life's way
Where do I get the words of prayer
That fill my heart each day
Where do I get the hope and faith
A far place I don't know
That fills me up with longing
As I watch the flowers grow
I am not alone in my wanderings
I am not alone in my pain
All I need to do is ask
And I will be filled again

THE RAVEN

I saw the raven sleek and black
I saw the raven's sneak attack
Upon a sparrow brown and grey
The sparrow is not here today

And the raven's sneak attack
Without anger, without wrath
With no malice or intent
The raven's hunger given vent

For only man will plan and scheme
In search of wealth in search of dream
And broach no change in his design
He dares fate to cross the line

And conscience will change him naught
As down the years they scheme and plot
As nature's way fulfills a plan
Unlike the self determined man

The flowers, fruit, and seed, then done
As in life, with man and son
As nature leaves a memory fair
But man may leave no flowers here

THE HOUSE WIFE

It really isn't hard to be a house wife
There really isn't very much to do
The days just follow one another
And there isn't really anything that's new

You leave your bed, each and every morning
At five or six, depending on the chores
Like getting all the folks to dress, and breakfast
Hunt boots, and books, and get them out of doors

And mothers hardly ever need a rest time
They like to wash, and clean, and cook, and shop
And when evening comes, they just keep right on working
It isn't likely that they'll want to stop

And now we get to all the little people
For after prayers, and storybooks are read
She likes to take the mending and the sewing
And finish it before she goes to bed

REGRETS

Yesterday is dead and gone, did you use it well?
Were there deeds you hid from view, and things you could not tell
Were your thoughts just for yourself of things you could acquire
To fill your day and fill your nights, with all that you desire
Or did you shed a tear or two, for someone on their way
Who had far less to fill their heart, and needed help today

And did you share the word of hope, to lighten and renew
And did you give a helping hand, a little part of you
For goodness is a spreading force, it cannot be denied
The golden light of goodness, a light you cannot hide
Go do some worthy deed today, before the sun has set
Tomorrow you won't have to feel, yesterday's regret

CHARACTER

I wish the words I said, I could recall
The hurtful words, the cutting tone and all
Replace them with thoughts I later had
The fact that I cannot, is very sad
If I could just relive that time again
To keep my tongue in cheek, and count to ten
No one would know the thought I had in mind
My smile, my countenance would give no sign
For I would keep my true self in reserve
And gain a favoured thought, I don't deserve
As I enjoy your adulation
Which now would be my reputation
All who know would now infer
I have a sterling character

THE LOST LADY

I see in distant past, a girl
Who smiled, and felt, and wept
Who wrote of wonders everyday
In diaries that she kept

And when I take the key and read
Vague feelings churn, and stir
And pictures of a smile I see
What has become of her?

There are no ties to bind
No anchor to hold tight
The years can sever silver cords
By just our losing sight

And one day sadness tells it all
No words can speak our mind
Or pictures of this other world
That we have left behind

And all the painful memories
Won't tell us what we were
And even mirrors do not show
What has become of her?

LOST ONE

I am all my ears have heard
And all my eyes have seen
And I am all the things I've done
And everywhere I've been
And I am bound with hurt and pain
The feelings of each day
And I am shaped by actions
And every word you say
My time is coloured by my thoughts
Of what you think of me
Just a shadow of myself
That's what I seem to be
But somewhere standing off alone
A figure I don't know
An eager human entity
Waiting just to grow
As I am pushed to bend and sway
And lose myself just in between
What I am, or might have been

THE DIET

It's chocolate bars, and cake, and ham
That really makes me what I am
My hips and thighs each day expand
With eating fresh, and fried, and canned
And never wasting ere a crumb
But eating all, the total sum
I didn't think I'd rue the day
By letting cookbooks have their way
I read each page, each recipe
And made them all, and ate with glee
And then I read a diet book
It told me how I'm gonna look
But Oh! I have so far to go
Before I see my feet below
And so I started, just today
And on my plate the lettuce lay
A grapefruit and a carrot stick
Oh! Watch the clock, and hear it tick
I weighed myself, and I'm the same
In fact, I think there's some small gain
What if I lose and they don't care
What if they cannot see me here
It's been so hard on my first day
But if I eat what will they say
It's chocolate bars, and cake, and ham
That really makes me what I am

COMMON SENSE

I wander in the wilderness of mind
As I am lost in thought
Involved in past shadows
Plagued with memories unsought

Confronted with the vague unfamiliar
Faded, distant past
That strikes a cord, resounds
Sometimes clings fast

I hear myself in soundless words
I see myself of long ago
A mosaic of differences
Of dreams, of happiness and woe

I tuck these memories
And all the hurts aside
Attribute these to ramblings
And say the tears have lied

But truth looms like a wall
There written, all the black deeds past
I must confront the bygone days
And study them in form and mass

And I have changed, but still
The shadow me, will linger near
To warn and show me what can be
If I don't plan with care

But will I heed the warning voice
And practice common sense
Or will I reach to hold the hand
Of consequence

BIRTHDAY

When you were just a little one
I held you on my lap
I sometimes fed you baby food
I watched you take your nap
And now you hold a baby
And live his baby days
Can you see a bit of me
In all his baby ways
And so the world keeps turning
With crib and baby chair
And he may bring me back to mind
Some day when I'm not here
And we in life can ask no more
That he may let me stay
Within your heart as special
When I am far away

WHERE I AM

Where am I gone the girl I was
I saw her yesterday
Or was it in the distant past
She gently slipped away

All lost in what she was to be
To everyone around
Her eyes brim full of misty dreams
That never cleared the ground

So busy all her lifetime
With all there was to do
Like vapour in her minutes spent
She's finally lost to view

And drifts among the days and years
Unseen by everyone
And toils, and works, and worries thus
From dawn to dying sun

And when they do not need her
They leave and go their way
She's left with just her dusty dreams
Close by her where she lay

WHEN I WAS YOUNG

When I was oh so very young, my tongue was sharp and glib
I stamped upon, and shouldered through, all I thought and did
I never even looked behind, or lost a sleepless night
I revelled in each moment spent, in each new days delight
The past was soon forgotten, nor was it brought to mind
The things I learned not woven in the future years design
I felt no need to dwell upon, my past mistakes or woe
Or draw from these examples in the paths that I should go
And so the years were eaten up, in greedy days of time
I looked not right or glanced to left, nor saw the warning signs
Then suddenly my time was spent, I felt each past regret
I searched my thoughts but found no help in ghosts I'd layed to rest
And so now weary and unsure, without a guiding hand
My days just seem to slip away, in hourglass of sand
And even though I'm old and wise, and everything is clear
I could tell folks how to live, but no one wants to hear

PRIVATE INTERLUDE

I saw her eyes grow distant
Expression leaves the face
She travelled far back into time
She fingered shawl and lace

And she was lost in memories
In days of long ago
In hurt, and pain and lost loves
In things I didn't know

And so I dropped my worried gaze
Not wishing to intrude
She left me for a little while
In private interlude

And the quiet filled the waiting
The loneliness my heart
It hurt to feel her live a life
I could not be a part

But suddenly I heard her sigh
Her countenance relax
She turned her gaze upon my face
I knew my love was back

And if I lose her for awhile
I'll wait, because you see
Maybe someday when I am gone
She'll dream of me

THE PLODDERS

There's lots of folks on earth like us
Who try our best, but miss the bus
Who work and worry round the clock
But find our boat has left the dock

But still each day we face ahead
Accepting what we get, instead
Of all the things we planned upon
And dream each night, then face the dawn

And pack our dreams to lay away
To take them out some future day
Undaunted, as we try each year
To act as if we do not care

And step ahead in time and space
To keep up with the human race
And suddenly we face the fact
We are this stranger, looking back

To someone that we lost back then
When we were twenty, we were ten
We only meant to pause awhile
But did not mean to change our style

The rut we carved, is strong and deep
We only dream when we're asleep
There's lots of folk on earth like us
Who carry on, and do not fuss

But ah! Our dreams are sweet and soft
We take them out and dust them off
But know our rut is strong and deep
And ever more will fit our feet

A WORD

A careless word can hurt the heart
And sometimes make the teardrops start
And spoil a day, and lose a friend
And leave us lonely in the end

If only we would think awhile
The words we say so sharp with guile
Retract and change to something nice
Not speak, before we think it twice

We'd make someone a happy day
Not chase some new found friend away
Good words are like the sun, they heal
They bless the heart and make us feel

So at the start, if we but learn
That what we say, in part return
And colour us for all to see
They weave our personality

THE WONDER

I wonder where the wonder went
For when I was a child
It shone like gold in all I saw
A promise all the while

Each year brought new surprises
A miracle each day
And filled my heart with wonder
As I skipped along the way

But shadows crept along the years
And chill winds blew despair
I lost the wonder of those times
I couldn't find it anywhere

But as I grew with time and thought
As wisdom changed my mind
A childlike splendour filled my days
It wasn't hard to find

For it had hidden in my heart
And waited there content
Until I took the time to find
Just where the wonder went

MY REVERIE

I close my eyes; accept the gentle gift of sleep
That ends the weary day
I drift and dream of wondrous things
And places far away

Then I am all I wish to be
In any place I deem
No trouble touches this my heart
When I lie down and dream

I do not smell the flowers
But join them in their bed
And speak to birds up in the sky
Though not a word is said

And when the sun of morn invades my sleep
And seeks my reverie to take
I hold this elusive slumber if I can
For I don't want to wake

THE ANGEL

An angel came to our house
To stay a little while
Her eyes are dark, her hair is soft
She has a lovely smile

And I am here to help her
Until some future time
When she will grow, and she will leave
She isn't really mine

I am just her guardian
She's owned by God above
The only thing that I may take
Is just her love

SOFTLY

I see the trees, and it makes my heart sing
I see willows flow, as they grow in the spring
I feel soft warm rain, as it covers the ground
And drops on my heart, with its rhythmical sound

Like the beat of a drum, like the sound of a fife
Above and around me, the music of life
I marvel at nature, the growth of a tree
Is all of this beauty just put here for me

For when I'm alone, when no one is around
My heart beats with life, a wonderful sound
And if I were to die in this moment of time
When all of this earth and myself are in rhyme

And I am content, and in the right place
With love in my heart, and a smile on my face

I'll go softly

WHITE RIVER

Quiet river cold and white
Waiting here like me

Quiet river cold and white
When will you be free

When the sun will gaze on her
On some future day

The cold and white will disappear
And she will run away

A HIDDEN GARDEN

A hidden garden with a wall
Where no one else can see
With only flowers as my friends
All else will let me be

Where I can let my dreams escape
Or maybe rest or sleep
Where the soft breeze sings a lullaby
And only clouds can peep

A hidden garden with a wall
To close the whole world out
And flower friends, and fairy elves
To see what I'm about

SOMEWHERE ELSE

Do you believe in somewhere else
Where flowers never die
Where you can talk to animals
And giant turtles fly

Do you believe in somewhere else
Where you are all alone
Except for thoughts within your head
That tell of the unknown

Do you believe in somewhere else
Where fluffy clouds on high
Are really boats that sail away
Across the sea blue sky

Do you believe in somewhere else
I tell you if you do
You'll live a life with treasures rare
As all we dreamers do

WHEN THEY ARE GONE

When I come home from work each night
I sit beside the fire bright
With children round, and on my knee
Their faces filled with trust I see

It scares me just a little bit
To think they will not always sit
That someday they will go away
When they are grown, and cannot stay

Alone beside the fire bright
I stare into the flames alight
With empty arms and empty knees
But a heart that's full of memories

COME I NEED YOU

Someone so sweet and gentle
Someone so kind and good
Who always did the best for us
In every way she could

No matter what the trials
Whether big or small
With mother's understanding
Took them all

She gave guidance when we faltered
She gave hope when times were bleak
And with mother's love she gave us strength
When we were spent and weak

And we took it all for granted
Until the very day
The Lord said, "Come, I need you."
And took our mom away

I MISSED YOU

I had quite a day today
The moment that you went away
I made the beds and did the dishes
Mended all with many stitches
I miss you
Did the wash, built the fire
Watched your PJ's go round in the dryer
I miss you
I lunched alone, what did you do?
My lonely lunch that's nothing new
My afternoon is fully booked
I have to clean, I have to cook
I miss you
I try all things to fill the space
And all these minutes, what a waste
This whole long day, has been a bore
But finally I hear the door
I missed you

THE NIGHTINGALE

I hear the song of the nightingale
Sweet on the summer air
And I close my eyes and listen
As it sings away my care

They sing to me of the wonders
They know of the clouds on high
And they sing of their tomorrow
Not afraid of that day, like I

For each new dawn brings promise
And each new night repose
For all the birds that fly the sky
For all of nature knows

But I look at my future
As if the sun has set
And all my days are shadows
Deep grey with past regret

It's only when the nightingale
Sweet on the summer air
I glimpse a bright tomorrow
As he sings away my care

WONDER LAND

Always in the shadows, no one knows my name
Always on the fringe of things, never in the game
Never felt the sunlight on my bended head
Never had the chance to lead, always being led

Doing what the others do, mouthing every word
Living life believing everything I heard
Life would spin its curtain without a single flaw
I never questioned anyone, or anything I saw

But when I grew in wisdom, when I was very old
I saw the world as others did, I questioned what was told
But I'm glad I slept so long and deep, I'm glad that I took care
To live in such a wonder land, and just see beauty there

SORRY JOE

Oh heaven help this heart of mine
To love her though I know
That she belongs to someone else
I'm awful sorry Joe

The tricks were mean, and not quite fair
Of that my mind does know
I took her in an unfair fight
I'm awful sorry Joe

I had a car I played it hard
My head is bending low
I took her out when you were gone
I'm awful sorry Joe

But it's all done we're married now
And you feel bad although
She was your girl, and you loved her
I'm awful sorry Joe

She's mean and nasty yes sir'ee
Its wedding bells and so
I married her, you lucky guy
I'm awful sorry Joe

RICH

I entered life through troubles door
And did not know that I was poor
My head was filled with hopes so high
And lovely visions filled my eye

I listen to the birds that sing
And beat the summer air with wings
I listen to all nature's call
And I could only marvel at the wonder of it all

THE CHANGELESS HEART

If you would take me as I am
With all my faults, and want me still
When I am bad, and I am good
When I am being strong of will
When I have no redeeming grace
And even angels shield their eyes
You stay because you cannot go
For I am where your future lies
Now only can you say you care
In truth your eyes will tell me so
And pain will paint a weary face
If I would say I have to go
But love's a word so often spoke
Dropped glibly from an easy tongue
And used in phrase and poetry
And set to music often sung
I want no part of lips that speak
The easy words all crave to know
But wait for truth, and feelings
A heart that means, I love you so

THE SOLDIERS

Side by side we lie in silent sleep
The hush that fills the ear came suddenly
No sound of drum, or bugle call
Disturbs our final reverie

Side by side no longer enemies
Who fought for such a little land to keep
Now know each others hearts and minds
And dream the weary battles in the deep

But no one hears or heeds our anguished cry
The battle rages on above, and see
More death, and pain, more broken souls
As we become a page in history

SCULPTOR'S CHOICE

When I was three, I wasn't me
But some unknown, a little child
I had not joined the human race
But walked life's road in single file
Without a thought to call my own
I was but then a piece of clay
To mold by those who held my time
Who shaped the minutes of my day
I could have been so many things
But I am now the sculptor's choice
I walked the road a pre-mapped route
For in my time I had no voice
But then there are the quiet times
When at a distance I can see
Within my mind, within my heart
A shadow that could set me free
The clay is soft, and would remold
What would this sculptor make of me?
This restless soul, this searching heart
Would wish to make a brand new start
But I am molded as I am
And even though I search and yearn
I am patterned like as man
And know that three cannot return

GOOD THOUGHTS

My world of thought is clear precise
I only think of things real nice
The weather here is always fair
With flowers growing everywhere

And everyone I meet is friend
With roads that gently curve and wend
To cottages all shuttered small
Tucked in beside a forest wall

And all is well that ends my day
With crystal stars that show the way
And golden moonlight acres deep
To end my thoughts in quiet sleep

BUT LOVE

I search through the darkness of days, for my love
But even the sunshine hides all feeling
The journey is so long alone
Successive years come softly stealing

Words need to be threaded together like pearls
Worn proudly around the milk white throat of days
Never to be mistaken as anything else but love
Seen by all, in shining eyes, in attitudes and ways

HIDDEN FOE

Hold me till my tears are dry
If it takes a hundred years
Help me share this pain I feel
Say the things I want to hear

Sadness is a hidden foe
Plunging us in deep despair
It's a trip to Neverland
No one ever likes it there

But we do not choose our fate
Our hearts choose, we know not why
Will you love me everyday
Or hold me till my tears are dry

GREY CLOUDS

My heart, like endless sunless days
Despairs of ever feeling warm
It lies like grey clouds, distant, cold
All sullen like a coming storm

To stir my thoughts and spill my tears
To churn life in this empty soul
There is no love but empty mind
To make this youth feel barren old

It seems I face the time alone
And I have aged in just a day
As oldness seeps in every bone
With letting grey clouds have their way

THE PARTING

Tears of release won't fall
But rest in my throat to stay my words
In this condition nothing sweet is heard

I stand sentry to each day
Not seeing the rise or set of sun
Nor hear the silver river run

In my body prison bound
Is darkness silent numbing cold
This passing time till I am old

There must be some small spark of hope
Some magic potion I can take
Unless there is, I'll never wake

For love in life, like fire must be fed
And built upon, enlarged, and dreamed
For time is just a minute seemed

With love the minutes stretch to years
Each day a lifetime spent
And age creeps up unknowingly
With all the kisses lent

We journey into sightless bliss
As love with all her guile
Will take our years, and part us soon
But only for awhile

TROUBLED MIND

I do not search my troubled mind
I could not be so brave
Because the past is hidden there
All things both sad and grave

And in the corners, in the dark
Past things I have forgot
Regrets, dead loves, and bitter words
And things that hurt a lot

So I've devised a way of life
That seems to fit my need
I laugh a lot, and keep it light
I'm always in the lead

But there are times this does not work
When things don't turn out right
Sometimes when I am all alone
And in the dead of night

Then I must face my true self
These times I cannot lie
I see myself for what I am
And lay alone and cry

But when the morning turns to day
I smile, with head held high
You'd never know I can't forget
That lonesome by and by

MY TIME

My days are mostly waiting
I rest and pause to see
What I can do, what use am I
And what they now expect of me

But I have hidden thoughts
Dreams of my very own
I look at and examine
When ever I'm alone

Someday I hope not far away
I'll spend time as I may
And enter into my dream world
Not live from day to day

But feel and know the me I hide
Beneath what seems to be
In what I do for others
Instead of just for me

My life seems now a waiting time
A capsulated spell
A story of unfinished days
I've yet to tell

BE CAREFUL

Be careful what you think of
Be careful what you say
For all our words, and all our thoughts
Come back to us someday

And no amount of wishing
Will erase the memory
For they will haunt your days and nights
And color all you see

And if you have been sometimes kind
The scales will balance out
Gentle thoughts and actions
Will show what you're about

Our deeds and words like shadows
Will filter through our days
And visit us in dead of night
And be with us always

HIGH ON A HILL

High on a hill where the wind blows free
I hold up my head and it tosses me
I close my eyes so I cannot see
And I sigh

I feel reborn clean and tall
I can't remember a worry at all
And all I can hear is a whippoorwill call
And I cry

Now I am a person proud and pure
Now I am a person with lots in store
All is gone that was before
And I sigh

WHERE I WANT TO BE

Just where the hawk can travel
That's where I want to be
Up where the mind can sail away
Just where the eye can see
Over the green wood flying
Over the green wood sea
Just where the eagle travels
Lord of his own domain
His company the quiet wilderness
His companions the wind and rain
Just where the grey wolf travels
Beneath the spruce and pine
A silent ghost of the forest
Beneath the mountain line
Just where God can see us
The birds, the wolf, and me
Accepting all of his blessings
That's where I want to be

D DAY

Oh for a smile from a vanished face
The touch of a hand that's still
The sound of my name from the silent lips
I can't hear, and never will

Oh for a word of kindness or pain
Or the sound of a hearty laugh
But there's only the stare of an ageless face
In a faded photograph

It's the story of feeling that has no end
And stays the same each day
A changeless, ceaseless pain of the heart
That never goes away

And we had such wonderful dreams and plans
As we faced each brand new dawn
And the years stretched happily far ahead
But now that future's gone

Will his going ensure a world that's free
And freedom for every man
Where is the prize he died for
Show me if you can

No one can lend me a helping hand
Even though they suffer like I
All I can hear is the voice of the lost
And the whispered question why

ALONE

I don't mind the aging, the falling of skin
Not seeing so good, the hair getting thin
But I miss most of all, the exchange of ideas
The words that I speak, if it falls on deaf ears
It seems it's a void that cannot be filled
For words linked together, this cannot be willed
Into great conversation, that fills heart and soul
More precious than jewels, when we're growing old
The greeting of friends, the passing of time
The words tumble forth, with no reason or rhyme
The sharing of feeling, that leaves a warm glow
And changes a stranger, to folks that we know
I don't mind the aging, but I don't understand
The unsmiling face, the clenching of hand
When just a small smile could brighten the day
To light up our path, as we go on our way
I don't mind the aging; it's folks that I've known
That have left, and I've stayed and I walk alone
I can laugh at the wrinkles, and ignore the fat
The ache in each bone, I'll handle that
But loneliness hurts, and silence is bleak
When you've shared all your life, and memories keep
To pull and to tug, and takes long to depart
And often just leaves a dull pain in your heart
I don't mind growing old, but I cannot abide
The last years alone with no one by my side
I'm walking my path, as my life would demand
If you see me, just smile, and offer your hand

MASKS

Everyday is Halloween
We see it on the streets each day
The masks we wear to hide ourselves
The jokes that cover what we say

The laugh that hides our inner selves
The tears we hold that do not fall
Each day to guard our hearts and minds
We wear our thick skinned overhauls

And inward crying, we reach out
But somehow cannot find the way
So hand and heart is empty
At the closing of the day

OH! LET ME KEEP

I love to wander down a dusty lane
Or rest beneath an old and sprawling tree
And from where I stand, no one has put a hand
To change a single thing, that I can see
Maybe, I'll just sit down here till tomorrow
And fill my heart with all that is around
And there is no chair that's made, not anywhere
As comfy as this little piece of ground
The trees flow like the curtains on a window
And no picture window had a better view
And the clouds up in the sky, soft and white, and high
Before the wind, are sailing in the blue
And suddenly, I hear a mellow, soft sound
A tiny cricket just above my ear
He sings his cricket song, so nothing can be wrong
I think he does it just because I'm here
And as I sit and take in every wonder
I am changed, and feeling something new
What are troubles I will say, that was another day
I am filled with hope, and love, refreshed anew
And when I leave, for I must go
To fill my time and place
Oh let me keep in memory
My day of grace

THE SEA

So like the bud upon the tree
I nestled in its waves
And floated over sunken ships
And long lost seamen's graves
And though my eyes were limited
My mind did soar on thought
I saw the death of many ships
Its hidden anger wrought
It ran along the shore with me
It sang a salty song
It told me tales of distant lands
All the summer long
It scolded me in anger
And tossed me in its scorn
It rapped me in its foggy mist
And lulled me with its horn
When it was quiet, gentle
As gentle as could be
It crept upon the sandy shore
And waved goodbye to me

LIKE YOU

Do not put a name on me, or voice my different race
Because I may be tall or short, the color of my face
Or think of me as separate, but only by my acts
If we must judge a way of life, judge only by the facts
Does not my heart beat just like yours, do I not dream like you
I search the future far ahead, and I have planned it to
Why think that I am different, look in my eyes and see
Hope and promises and dreams, you are the same as me
The air is shared by both of us; I walk the road like you
If you would look, then you would see, the many things I do
And I have love within my heart, a waiting hand unfilled
And friendship budding to burst forth, this may be lost and stilled
It only takes a second to forget the hurt and blame
Just a minute to reflect, that we are both the same
If all the different races, spread across the land
Could only see with, just the heart, then they would understand

Hilda Nightingale

LOVE IS NEVER OUT OF MIND

Where ere we tread this earth we find
That love is never out of mind

Like sunlight on a grassy plain
Like flowers searching for the rain

We cannot face the day alone
We need a love to call our own

And hand to hold to counter fear
To know that someone's standing near

All else is cold, but love will bind
So love is never out of mind

THE PAST

I made my bed all neat and new
And smoothed the counterpane
And watered all my indoor plants
Then watered them again

I'll dim the lights, and pull the shades
And sweep before I go
And stack the dishes on the shelf
The cups all in a row

But everything looks lonely
As if they know that I
Am straightening for the last time
Before I say goodbye

But I'll be back some future time
I've been through this before
I looked with longing at my past
Then turned, and closed the door

LIFE'S GOBLET

I will not mark the calendar today
But cling to all the minutes till the end
I cannot bear to see them slip away
The sunlight o'er the far off mountain bend
And though I love the velvet of the sky
At night alight with diamond studded star
I do not want to see my hours die
I want to keep tomorrow distant far
Oh how I love each minute that I spend
In viewing nature and all it unfolds
To every scene on life's stage I attend
Drinking of life's goblet, all it holds
And I am filled with love to overflow
And spend each day and night like silent gold
To seed the precious minutes there and grow
And fill my heart with every story told
And I have closed my eyes, and not seen time
But it has paced each step that I have trod
And silent smiled at my subterfuge
As father time did sit and wink and nod
And mirrors on the walls, showed up my ruse
And finally I must accept at last
That I have used up all my days
The costly years, and spent my past
But if I had to do it all again
Retrace each step, each joyous mile
Would I live a different life, or change a thing
Or just look back and smile

IS IT TOO LATE

Just a day of waves and sand
Seagulls calling, holding hands
Soft winds whispering in trees
Just a day of all of these

I never knew that I would feel
While seeing these, that I should kneel
I saw the future by the past
That I had time, and these would last

I see the crimson, golden fall
It seems the first that I recall
I never gave a word of praise
For all those lovely sunlit days

Until I knew that I would see
Maybe the end of all of these
I now give thanks for things so small
For things I didn't see at all

I know too late, and I feel pain
My tears will mingle with the rain
When time has come and we must part
We feel regret within the heart

Why didn't something set me free
To show what life could really be
It was all here just for my sake
I slept too long, but now awake

I see the truth, I know the lies
It took so long to make me wise
My life has filled my heart with pain
Is it too late to start again

UNUSED TIME

What happens to the days that go unused
We fool ourselves with some pretext or ruse
That we have filled our time with worthwhile deeds
And used our years to ensure our future needs

Is there a place, where unused minutes lay
And hours are protected from the fray
And kept so precious, that they may be
Still useable, by you and me

Only a fool will say he's had his worth
Of all his hours since his birth
And never felt a seconds waste
In retrospect, in memory traced

And no regrets to tinge his day
Of all the time he threw away
But truthfully can say that he
Spent everyday, as meant to be

I doff my hat, and bow my head
If he believes these words he said
For I procrastinate, and feign
For I would like that time again

THE WORLD

Protected by a picket fence
And roses on the door
She lived each day with happiness
And future years in store
With eyes all clear and sparkling
And heart upon her sleeve
She thought that everything in life
With dreams she could achieve
Outside the gate the world did wait
Dark clouds despair and pain
And if at first did not succeed
It waits to try again
To steal the wonder of her days
Her blissful hours spent
As life conspired all the while
To sow it's discontent
But what the whole world could not do
I alone did score
To take the stars and dreams away
The roses from the door
Dry eyed and old I see her stand
Though not a day has passed
She joined the faded multitude
Embraced this world at last

TELL HIS STORY

Take the name of Jesus with you
Tell His story everywhere
Share your faith with friend and stranger
Till we are together there

Brighten up the darkest corner
See God's love like light, shine through
Give, yes give to everybody
It will come right back to you

Sow the seeds of love and kindness
Plant them deep and let them lie
Just like seeds in any garden
They will grow and multiply

In our heart there is a heaven
It's for sinners, you and me
Would we spread God's loving word
The light would shine for all to see

Take the name of Jesus with you
Weary travellers we are
We need his help, his love, his kindness
For we have to travel far

351

THE LOVELESS

Father was so busy
That he didn't see the lad
Or the way he ran to meet him
Or how his face was glad

And when he tried to reach up
To the idol that he saw
He was repulsed at every turn
And the pain began to gnaw

And as the years were wasted
And all feelings buried deep
He hid the pain down in his heart
And then in dreams he'd seek

Fulfillment for his yearnings
Responses to his needs
And his days were fed and nourished
From the fruit of bitter seeds

And as he grew and reached out
His days were fraught with fear
He found he could not give or take
He could not bring love near

And so the rhythm of his days
Became a monotone
He joined the band of loveless souls
And spent his life alone

THE WAITING

I did not notice time had passed
Until I saw my children dear
The little girls so sweet and grave
Now had silver in their hair

And little lads who had my help
In years gone by, for that was when
I dressed, and washed, and counselled all
But just like that, have grown to men

I cannot say I saw them grow
Love crowded all, I did not see
But just like magic time went by
And they outlived their need for me

Oh, how this hurt to realize
That they could manage on their own
That they would leave to build their nests
And travel to that great unknown

The time that had so swiftly passed
Now hung so heavy all the day
And so I wait, in silent hope
Ever since they went away

To fill a need to be of help
To give before it gets too late
For time is stealing all my days
But still I wait, I wait

FOR I STILL LOVE

I didn't know a heart could break
From just an unkind act
But after years of this neglect
I know that it's a fact
Then how can I still feel for you
Beneath this heart of pain
So that each time you reach for me
I come right back again
Maybe I think that you have learned
Not that you're crass or weak
Maybe you just fulfill a need
When it's my hand you seek
Or maybe hope is all I have
And memories I have known
That make my days just liveable
Whenever I'm alone
And I refuse to see the truth
Just like a light ahead
I'd rather read the things I want
In all the things you said
But now I know a heart can break
A little at a time
As I relive the lies you told
Stored deep within my mind
I see no future to my life
Except that I might be
A little part of all your days
For I still love, you see

TWO OF US

It's just the two of us
Yes the two of us
It's the way it's supposed to be
Just the two of us
Yes the two of us
There's only you and me
As the years steal the days
And the rest go their ways
They leave the two of us
With a better love
Than it ever used to be
And each night I lay
Oh but first I pray
To thank the Lord for you
That I am part of the two
Of us

TIME JUST PASSES

Time just passes with no design
When will some of that time be mine
It's allotted to all around I see
I disperse it, though some belongs to me
I keep saying tomorrow I will be done
As I hear and see clocks tick and run
I feel gratification when I give my best
So I use my time for work not rest
But I dream of the wonderful days ahead
With all work done, and all words said
And I'll have leisure to spend as I may
In some distant year, on some quiet day
Oh what a wonderful time that will be
When I spend every second and minute on me
But how time flies, it swallows each year
As I see each day, and each week disappear
I see myself old, and all most through
I see my thoughts stagnate, and nothing is new
The years that have passed, have stolen my prime
I'm tired now, and there isn't much time
And the only thought that holds back the tears
Is I've been doing what's me, all of these years

THE LETTER

You left your tears on my letter
When I read it I saw on each line
That the girl that I loved was so lonely
That this girl was no longer mine

It's so sad that the days in each parting
Make strangers of each loving pair
And each seeks another for solace
When their partner is no longer there

And my heart ached as I read your letter
I saw the closing of so many doors
And my tears fell on this lonely letter
And blended on paper with yours

DOLLS

Dolls, all in a row with expectation on their faces
Big dolls, small dolls, dolls of all races
Owned by girls in training for motherhood
Telling their doll to sleep or be good
Feeding them, changing them, rocking to sleep
Kissing them, scolding them, don't make a peep
Taking them out for their morning walk
Dressed in their best, pretending they talk
A stroller, a carriage, or just loving arms
Stealing their hearts with their doll like charms
And the love small girls feel, is sincere and real
With the loss of a doll the heart doesn't heal
A mother's love is just the same
Even though it starts a game

HIDDEN THUNDER

Deep within my soul
I hide from everyone
All the evil thoughts I have
And all the bad things I've done

But up in front there is
A person you don't know
For I portray a good face
And purity bestow

My real self would be left
All lonely, so you see
I must present a portrait
That really isn't me

How many men in life
Would have to live alone
For they would be rejected
If they were truly known

And so we clothe ourselves
In raiment shiny bright
That we remove and fold
In darkness of the night

There is another world
Of guilt and wrongs, and blunders
That screams aloud, but no one hears
This hidden thunder

BY-ROADS OF THOUGHT

As I journey in unexpected places
On by-roads of thought
Through little lanes of dreams
Gifts of feelings not sought
Payments for my wanderings
Unaware adventures of tomorrow
And I am there in essence
Partaking of joy and sorrow
This fills me with sweet expectations
I become impatient with today
And fantasize with future revelations
On levels by touch with the heart
And all the words I lack
Are spent in soundless speech
I cannot take them back
Some I wish so to forget
Some hurt and bring me tears
I push them far back in my mind
But they came back down through the years
All the private thoughts of mine have been
Unexplored areas, and hidden places
Building visions and dreams
Wordless pictures of scenes and faces
And if I leave this quiet world
And come back to reality
I do not fit into this rut
So now what will become of me

AN OPEN MIND

I make up my mind, and think it's so
Of all the things I do not know
Deciding that, it must be right
When letting fancy take to flight
And so I travel on my way
Grow more aggressive with each day
I close my mind to outside thought
And every try avails me naught
And open mind with winds of change
An open heart with love arranged
Each day a mirrored image see
Will show how humble I should be
But will I heed that inner voice
Will I pause and make a choice
Will I change and mend my ways
Will I improve, with my last days
We must not let our time slip by
But give each day an honest try
Take the time to plant the seed
To sprout an honest, thoughtful deed

WHEN DREAMS ARE GONE

What will I do when my dreams are gone
What will fill my day
Will I notice the silver moon
As it shines upon the bay
Will my eyes be blind to all
The creatures the trees the sky
Not seen through the golden mist of dreams
That used to fill my eye
And what will I think but empty thoughts
Or feel with an empty heart
Will I be jaded like the rest
When I used to stand apart
And will I believe in a future
And better things ahead
With nothing to filter my days through
When all of my dreams are dead
For I cannot see the rest of my life
With no future dreams in store
For we cannot sail the boat of hope
If it never leaves the shore
We cannot feel life truly
If we do not dream or plan
A vision is a guiding light
To be seen by every man

I SEEK A LOVE

I seek a love just for myself
Someone to fit me right
Two eyes that I can sink into
Two arms to hold me tight

It doesn't happen just like that
No matter how it's sought
That we will find a love that fits
The way we think it ought

For feelings just can't be explained
No matter how we try
The reason two can feel as one
You just can't justify

And when the love is over
The pain is shared by two
And suddenly as strangers part
What will these lovers do

SWEET INNOCENCE

Dear sweet innocence, don't give your love so free
Don't lay your heart so bare, right there in front of me
For if I am unscrupulous, I'd take it all and run
I could say it all was play, and all in fun
Not look back and see the tears you shed
But forget today and only look ahead
I would not see your eyes grow cold
Or see your childlike face grow old
But only use your wonder and your laughter
And leave a shell for those who follow after

WINTER DAYS

There's no time left, no time at all
I've lived my summer, spring, and fall
And now the winter days have come
I treasure each and every one

I know how precious days can be
And all life's wonders I can see
Though age has shaped my outer frame
Still inward I remain the same

Accept the knowledge years have sent
It's kept within the heart and mind
I value all the days ahead
And treasure all the years behind

IT WOULDN'T BE THE SAME

Lonely hearts don't last for long
And lonely eyes will cry
And lonely ones will sit alone
But only for awhile

Lonely is slow dying
And tears run out from crying
And lonely ones will soon find out
Excuses are just lying

And through hurt and longing
We'll search for someone new
Or fall again for someone
Who looks a bit like you

But never give their whole heart
It hurt too much before
Just play at love and giving
To even up the score

And hope that you will see them
And hurt a little bit
That sleepless nights and heartaches
Is all you'll ever get

And even though revenge is sweet
It hurts her just to know
That maybe this here new love
Will keep him bending low

But if he comes back kneeling
And said it was a game
She'd take him back, and love him
But it wouldn't be the same

IN MEMORY

I cannot keep the fields of green
And every rose that I have seen
Imprisoned rainbows in the rain
But only bring them back again
In memory
I cannot hold the running brook
Or capture robin, lark or rook
I cannot catch the fleeting cloud
For only this may be allowed
In memory
I cannot hold those far away
I cannot make my loved ones stay
They fill my dreams each day somehow
But I can love and live them now
In memory

THE LEARNER

My smile may hide my heartache
I may not want to say
The things that hurt me deeply
For that was yesterday
And there are my tomorrows
And all that time ahead
To push back all the worries
And think of joy instead
No matter what the day or year
I've learned that time runs fast
And not to live out old regrets
For that was in the past
But keep it at a distance
And keeping it in mind
So we won't make the same mistakes
We choose to leave behind
And thus mature and move ahead
And in our time to see
Our worth, a pass, to rest awhile
In a better place to be

TRUE FRIEND

If it is true that we are friends
And linked together are our days
Hand in hand and heart to heart
Happily we walk the ways

Then I am fortunate indeed
To have someone so tried and true
And I will spend my time in thanks
Because I have a friend like you

LONGING

Longing is the turf of dreamers
A stroll through paths of mind
In hopes the answer to the longing
Is what they find

The quiet times of contemplation
Unlike life's cold embrace
Will stay and stir the heart
With each memory retraced

Longing like the heady thirst
Is never quenched for long
But only wets the heart for more
When the pull of life is strong

And so a momentary pause
A solitary, small retreat
To stay again the longing
To feel one's life complete

With the reaching and the searching
Some small measure is attained
For awhile, but know tomorrow
They feel longing once again

THE OLD GRAVEYARD

Tumbled down and grown with grass
The pickets missing here and there
But still the winds caress the stones
Murmurs that they cannot hear

The brambles thick beside the fence
As if to keep intruders out
But no one comes to bend a knee
There is no one to think about

The years have dried the lonely tears
The names are dulled and hard to see
Below are caskets, grey and bare
All the spirits have gone free

No more flowers placed above
And the mourners follow fast
Now all the names are memories
The circle has been closed at last

ONE DAY

My morning made of toast and tea
Of rising shades, so I can see
The garbage truck removes the can
With all the refuse made by man
But I will shade my eyes from this
And stare across the morning mist
A lively first, a new day scene
With shades of blues, and shades of green
With promises of things to come
A secret as to where they're from
I live each precious minute sent
Enjoying all, till I am spent
Then night will end the day for me
Till morning, and my toast and tea

Hilda Nightingale

LOVE IS ALWAYS THERE

What would life be without a thought
To start each minute sent
Making memories so sweet
To mark each day that's spent
In some forgotten time and place
And only brought to view
When warm love comes, and takes my mind
And leads my thoughts to you
Sometimes the words are not enough
And never can convey
The feelings that can fill a heart
When one is far away
Sometimes it takes the picture of
A long forgotten smile
The memory of a face so dear
That warms the heart awhile
Sometimes one may, just close their eyes
There is no need to see
It fills the heart with age old thoughts
And feeds upon past memory
And fans the embers laying there
Brings love to warm our day
It lights our path, and leads us on
And shows the way

THE MOLDER

You made me what I am today
I hope you realise
When hearts are soft and flesh is weak
They do not think of lies

So you can mold a rose or thorn
You have the choice you know
You can stunt a tender love
Or you can let it grow

The power that a love will have
When someone gives their heart
To hold it very tenderly
Or break it all apart

And just a word can do it
A moment of neglect
A callous way of living
Not stopping to reflect

There comes with love, a living trust
To have for just awhile
The precious moments, we can share
The rearing of a child

Hilda Nightingale

SAVING

I had a crust of bread one day
I didn't like to throw away
I put it in a pot to stew
It looked so plain, what could I do

I used some sugar and some cream
Instead of stew, I'll let it steam
I added raisins, nuts, and fruit
And salt and spices, just to suit

And soda so that it would raise
And covered it to let it laze
It took me nearly half a day
But I didn't throw that bread away

TODAY'S BEAUTY

She walks in beauty like the night
I stay indoors, I am a sight
My bust and hips defy the style
I plan to diet in awhile
The fashion magazines will say
I should be tall and thin today
And I, in shame stay home and hide
For I'm too short, and I'm too wide
But I feel good inside of me
The part that no one else can see
I'm trim and sleek, and pert and gay
And wear the fashions of the day
And even though they pull and tug
They don't fit here, and there are snug
I guess we are just who we are

I think I'll have a candy bar

THE TRAIN

I know now, why the sound of a train
Makes my man's heart leap with joy
For I remember the big black train
When I was just a boy
And how I'd wave when they flew past
And receive a responding hand
Oh how I envied the engineer
And the brakeman oh so grand
For it was a giant of hissing steam
That drew the cars behind
Along the rails and up the hills
Along the tracks that wind
But best of all was the whistle that blew
I'd listen until it died
And it left a feeling that stirred my soul
A feeling I can't describe
But it left a feeling stirred my soul
That's still here, deep inside

MY PAST

What am I doing here and now
When, with a backward glance I see
A time, a place, and just a thought
Can beckon and I long to be
Maybe nostalgia's all it is
That wistful print of memory
But, why my heart will jump with joy
With every thought that comes to me
Because the future is not seen
The present does not please the mind
We seek to live our yesterdays
By holding close the tie that binds
But, in truth by going back
To search the dreams we threw away
We will not find our future hopes
In some forgotten yesterday

Hilda Nightingale

THERE IS A PATH

There is a path ahead I see
That leads to peace but not for me
The roads that branch into despair
The rocky roads you'll find me there

The sun may shine upon your head
But mine will find the rain instead
For you the birds their sweet refrain
My ear will listen all in vain

And time soft time will treat you fair
But pass me daily unaware
For you see roses as you walk
And there's music when you talk

The world can be polite or rude
For life is but an attitude

A BRAND NEW START

Examine every morsel each minute of each day
And study every nuance
As they travel on their way
If head and heart were open
While standing straight and tall
Attuned to life's abundance
Then they would not mind at all
Whatever is forth coming
Would flow into the heart
And they could face the future
With a brand-new start

WHEN YOU WERE JUST A BOY

Do I know when you are gone?
My heart will break in two
The shadows of a long lost past
Will visit me anew
And will I mourn the happy days
That filled my days with joy
When I was very very young
And you were just a boy
To late to say that I still love
Each minuet that I live
Each day my heavy heart would ache
With all I had to give
I feel that distant yesterday
As if it were so real
And hold and live with shadows
For this is how I feel
But time may dull the corners
Each day with pain define
And fade the lonely minuets
The years your love was mine
Until I may look back upon
A faded memory
And stir cold ashes of the past
And find that I am free

GOOD LORD

When did I stop seeing rainbows?
Or feel the call of the day
Or notice a tree waving to me
As the minuets slipped away

When did I walk on the flowers?
Not notice the sun or the rain
Or take time to heed somebody in need
But just walk on again

When did I not hear nature?
When she beckoned and called to me
With a bird for my ear, a rose for my nose
And all those wonders to see

When I did not take time to count blessings
Or share a smile or a hug
My eyes did not see when I thought about me
And forgot the good Lord above

SHADOW DANCE

Shadows dance away the day
They sing with sunlight on their way
With pattern notes on walk and wall
Until they hear the evening call

Then shadows steal away and hide
Beneath beyond away inside
And wait to hear the morning call
To dance away the day with sol

THE OLD DAME

Within this wrinkled hide you'll see
A girl you used to know
She thinks the same and feels the same
The same get up and go

And though the years just slide on by
Her hopes and dreams remain
The things she did when she was young
She'd like to do again

And though they think her far too old
To ever dance the jive
She sees herself do that and more
It makes her feel alive

She does something oh! Now and then
That gets a youthful frown
And wears the clothing that she likes
That sometimes may astound

She's living life without regret
Her heart and mind are free
She grabs each day and wrings it out
The way that life should be

MOTHERS WORK

Defenders of the hearth
The battle lines are drawn
As sentinels a guard kept
From black of night till dawn

And through the daylight hours
When time is fraught with fear
Though out of sight and out of mind
The heart is always near

No Purple Heart or merits
For loving duty done
A mother wears her heart with pride
Until her years are done

HAPPINESS FLIES

The music in my soul is gone
My heart no longer sings
And all the beauty flies away
As if my days had wings

To some place dark and lonely
To lay alone and bare
Forgotten in the stillness
Without a thought or care

And time spins out unknowingly
The days of my neglect
I hold the hand of darkness
And dwell upon regret

It is too late to start
To follow sun drenched paths of mind
With just a change of heart

A DAY FOR ME

I have a reason to wake with the dawn
To open my eyes, to stifle a yawn
To look to the day all rosy and new
The garden a promise all covered with dew

As I lay abed and I make a plan
To use every minuet as best as I can
For today is a gift and it's given to me
From the dawn as it rose till it sinks in the sea

Within this time as it sheds its warm glow
I live love and feel all the things till I know
And I gather together a bouquet of thoughts
And feelings and dreams this new day has brought

Till minutes are spent like a magical wand
I am but feelings though day may be gone

NO CHANGE

Mothers never seem to tire
They like helping others it seems
They cook they wash they worry
And can even smile while they clean

And after the supper is over
And dishes are high in the sink
It seems company knows they have somewhere to go
And they leave with a smile and a wink

The day may leave mother weary
Each hour was filled with a zing
Next time that they come she'll be happy
And learn that she won't change a thing

ALL BEAUTY

Whence came these words upon my lips?
They are not mine
They hearken from some distant world
Some other time

If I was versed to know this day
And hold it tight
I'd fall in love
And pass it on when time was right

Not when my heart is cold
My eyes are filled with duty
But when each word is love
And all I speak is beauty

A DOGGONE WISH

I'd like to be a spaniel
For I know that people care
They feed and buy them doggy treats
And brush and comb their hair

I can easily sit and beg
I do it all the time
It's just that no one seems to see
I even sit and whine

When I am jogging to loose weight
My tongue will loll and drip
Though I do not stop at hydrants
And I do not bark or nip

At night some soul will worry
And shake and fix their bed
And say goodnight with great concern
And pet and stroke their head

ECHOES OF THE MIND

There is a place inside of me
Where echoes rest until disturbed
Then call their needs in plaintive voice
Till every single memories heard
Some ring with truth like silken bells
But some lay quiet and ashamed
And left to lay in darkness there
Not recognized and left unnamed
But good sweet ringing echoes tell
Of times gone by they tell the dream
The unnamed echoes could not mar
And could not seem to dull the sheen
And where to this place and to this day
Still undisturbed in shadows deep
Are echoes that recall in time
The aching heart their every beat
As hearts are true to time and space
And days of hope they soon deplete
Except where echoes stir the past
And memories spring to fill the mind
The silver bells will seem to ring
And leave the echoes far behind

IMPATIENT DREAMS

When winter comes it turns my thoughts to unhappy things
I no longer think in pictures of flowers and swings
I seem to sink to the depts. Of despair
Without my summer vision here

Why can't I delight in soft falling flakes?
That make silver trees, adorn fence and gate
Adjust to the time I may dream and rest
Of the future that brings flower and nest

A time for my heart to be grateful and glad
To thank God for the year I already had
And know in His wisdom He deemed it to be
A short resting time for each flower and tree

For spring will assure the cycle will start
All last years' abundance to gladden the heart
But I'm a mere human impatient with greed
Can't wait Mother Nature to answer my need
But sink into dreams of what next year will be
The gift and the glory of flower and tree

MISLED

And so the forces said
You must achieve and climb
I look down from dizzy heights
That never were in mind

I search the distance for myself
Befuddled and abused
That I could be so falsely led
In things I did not chose

But that was years ago and now
The voices in my head
Tell me with bitter nagging thoughts
That I was pushed and led

Down roads that held no vision
Within my heart and eye
So sweet with guile the voices
I did not hear the lie

NIGHTS CURTAIN

Draw night's curtain dark and soft
And hold the moon and stars aloft
I am now, I am me
Not dreams but real reality

I feel the thoughts that rapture lends
I see the past that memory sends
Alone to court the words unsaid
And walk the paths that dreams lead

Seduced again in nightly play
I put aside a work worn day
As night times curtain dark and soft
Still holds the moon and stars aloft

SORROWS

At the edge of my dream there's a shadow of you
And a memory that will not die
There's a vision I cannot seem to evade
No matter how hard I try

And they play on my heartstrings a melody sad
A haunting and tearful refrain
They're singing me notes I don't want to hear
But I hear them again and again

Neath the hum of the day and the silence of night
It plays on and on with it's theme
And if my eyes close and I fall asleep
It plays on again in my dream

So there's no place to go from this sorrow
And no place to go from this pain
While looking for someplace to shelter
The melody's playing again

SPRING FLOWERS

My gardens dead and dying
With leaves upon the ground
And nothing there to grace the eye
When I look around

And memory has failed me
There's nothing that I see
To help me to recall
What my garden used to be

And only when I walk along
And search each tiny nook
That I see signs of crocus
Beside the frozen brook

I say that I can't wait that long
To see a nodding head
Or tulip lily daffodil
In each and every bed

And oh my heart is gladdened
For when I look around
I see them all just peeping through
And waiting in the ground

STANDING BY

When the evening settles
And the lights are burning low
I would not change this place I have
With anyone I know

When the night is quiet
I've a feeling so content
I wonder at the peace I feel
And where the worries went

I stop to count my blessings
And what a joy they bring
God seems to touch the weary heart
And make the angles sing

And when I am complacent
And forget this wondrous day
I know that if I ask Him
God will show the way

And there may come another time
When things may go awry
I have the strength to face it
When God is standing by

THE LEAVES

Yes there alive alive I say
These whirling shapes of tan and brown
Some dance a waltz and some a jig
While others skip along the ground

They run and play like hide and seek
And pass away before my eye
So joyful seems they do not know
They are a gift no gold can buy

But soon their dance is winter still
Their gayest dance will cease to be
And there prevails sadness here
As I am left with barren tree

And hope that looking forward brings
For all will change and all renew
When nature sends another spring
And we will have a greener view

THE OLD LADY

An old and tired woman
Just sitting in her chair
Not offering opinions
For that she would not dare

And if a smile would play her lips
A spark would seek her eye
She lives another far off dream
That never seems to die

Those moments would sustain her
And feed her aching heart
She lives her life with shadows
In which she takes no part

MY WINTER TIME

I remember back to spring
The yesterdays of long ago
With childish thoughts and childish games
That left me with their after glow

But faded into summertime
When living was no game at all
The sharpness of each passing day
With hurt and pain I now recall

And as I changed from tenderness
To weary traveler in time
Each thought and deed were strange to me
I did not know them then as mine

But as the summer days depart
The autumn days my thoughts confine
And I am gentile once again
And softly live my winter time

ACROSS TIME

I remember golden days
That warmed my heart with golden rays
The faith I felt your hand in mine
And love was good and life was fine

I was now a butterfly
And splendor painted gold my wings
In loves warm glow in blackest night
I could hear the angles sing

And I could now ascend the sky
Where at a glance I saw the land
All flowers soft and diamond dew
And still you loved and held my hand

There was all the golden glow
The perfect love and just for me
That warmed my heart and let me know
Was here for all eternity

STERNER STUFF

I may be made of sterner stuff
Than folks I meet today
They do not know just what they want
Or seem to know their way

There courting indecision
As if it were a friend
And time is used unwisely
As if it had no end

And no one counts their blessings
For all the things they see
Perhaps they find no value
Because all nature's free

Each day they're in a hurry
And most folks have lost heart
We should not take each day as whole
But take it "a la carte"

SOUL SONG

Be to me the silver moon
The soft breeze of a summer day
Be the sun and warm my heart
Judge me not but see my need
Hold my love if you be wise
It is all of me and so
Read it deep within my eyes
It is now forever more
From sky to earth
From shore to shore
In words this feeling can't be told
But kept within my heart and soul

FUTILITY

Dust lies upon my memory
And softens pain
The long lost sharpness of reality
Won't come again

But still I long for the touch of it
So clear so sharp
Something that's mine alone to hold
So close to heart

The tears and lonely nights
Beneath the dust
That buried
All the hope and trust

The pineing and the ushered tears
Beneath the mantle that love wears
And seems to be the only part of me
That does not accept this exercise in futility

MARRAGE FIFTY-FIFTY

Marriage fifty-fifty
Well I guess I'd have to say
It was not true in days gone by
And it is not true today
Sometimes it's sixty –forty
Sometimes it's even more
We cannot see tomorrow
And what it has in store
Sometimes it's ninety-eight and two
I know it is with me
Sometimes it's straight one hundred
And it seems it has to be
But we should get things straightened out
Right before we start
You cannot run a marriage with just your mind
Its heart
Our marriage is fifty-fifty
And will be until the end
For he earns all the money
That I go out and spend

SHADOWS ON MY HEART

My days are withered up and gray
And covered up with useless wrath
Walked on with all my minutes tred
Vanished with the sunlight's path

And shadows will come back again
Conditions and the timing right
And darken corners of my soul
If I could but hold love so tight

And keep the sunlight days in thought
Then let the shadows play their part
When those shadows come again
To lay their fingers on my heart

A LOVE NO MORE

Our love is no more
And never will be
I said to you
And you said to me
And all was gone
On that final day
As you turned about
And I walked away
And the days of laughter
The touch the sigh
Were too good to last
And were bound to die
Consoled by friends
And folks that knew
That a love that dies
Cannot be true
And I was lucky
No harm was done
Someday I'll meet
My only one
And then
A great affair will start
If I could just convince my heart

THE SEA RAN ON

The sea ran on the sand
And washed the rocks in rhythmic sound
And makes a note as they recede
A song of surf its notes abound

And waves the seaweed to the shore
So like lace to dress the tide
And as it ran with melody
I heard the seagulls piping cry

I sat upon a silver log
And did not say a word
My heart was filled with wonder
With all I saw and heard

Hilda Nightingale

THE LIE

Footsteps only I can hear
That leads me on without a care
I follow with no will at all
The echoes in my ear

Footsteps resound with each new day
The music I will dance away
Not heading heart, and find
I have gone astray

Time steals all and does not cry
Apologize or tell you why
It sings it's cruel song
The melody is long "the lie'

GRAY DAYS

When I have fears
That I shall be no more
No warmth of hand
No friendly door
And when I look ahead
The days are gray

And all I've known
Has faded far away
And love sweet love
No longer touches me
All shadows now
And distant memories

CLOCKS

No one hears their heart
With it's dull aching beat
They must step aside
Like the chaff from the wheat

So just like a shadow
They silently stand
Out of step out of time
Not part of the band

But years give them hope
The patience to wait
They won't take rejection
As part of their fate

Time is so precious
And stanch as the rocks
They wait hearing only
The ticking of clocks

STORY

I listen to the story
Of the wind against the pane
And I ache with foreign feelings
When I hear a distant train
And it's just as if it's coming
From a far off distant land
And I'm filled with mixed emotions
That I do not understand

When I sit and listen
Then to contemplate
A feeling that is urgent
That now I am too late
It puts me in a quandary
A different state of mind
As if there is some place to go
And something I must find

I'm changed and now have choices
I face myself and see
Those quiet inner voices
The other part of me
And so the wind and train
And echo drift away
The memories and feelings
Have their way

HAND IN HAND

I dreamed of walking hand in hand
Through darkened days and weeks of pain
And thought I had the strength to cope
If it was asked of me again

And though it was a tangled dream
I knew it not nor saw ahead
That I had lived in dream like trance
Till all the bitter words were said

This fool would seek a place to hide
A hidden place to be alone
All dark and quiet without thought
And to all others be unknown

But I encountered multitudes
Of crying eyes and broken hearts
Of giving up and seeking strength
Among the rubble brand new starts

I did not dream that it was known
To all the distant shadows there
I thought this pain was mine alone
Not something I would have to share

But I can see reflected
In the shadows by my side
My pain, my hurt, my longing
That the others cannot hide

And soon we travel on in time
Though no plans may be laid
The minutes use us as they want
Till pain will fade

DREAM KEPT

There is a castle oh! So high
Atop a mountain in the sky
Its windows glisten on the sun
And with the moon when day is done

I often dream that I will see
The king hold out the golden key
So I might climb and enter there
And sit upon the golden chair

We dream as children you and me
And always hope that this will be
There are no doubts to cloud our mind
The paths we choose our feet will find

The road of days and years it takes
To wait until the dreamer wakes
If at the very end of time
We see the castles in our mind
With golden windows in the sun
And dreams still warm when life is done

JUST BECAUSE YOU CARE

I wake up in the morning
And there's flowers everywhere
And it does not really matter
If the weather is not fair

It comes about within my heart
A cheerful happy mood
And I can have just what I want
By change of attitude

For I am master of each day
And choose the gifts I deem
Why would I choose a nightmare?
When I can have a dream

There is beauty in each minute
And sunlight everywhere
I can live my life in hope
Just because you care

CANDLES

Reality is cold and so
I like to bask in candle glow
It seems to cleanse the weary day
And make the wobblies go away

It calms the senses like good wine
I like the candles when I dine
They throw long shadows on the wall
And lead my mind to chance recall

Times past that please in memory
The dreamy pictures that I see
Reality is cold and so
That's why I like the candle glow

MATURITY

I am a child though old and gray
I've traveled far from yesterday

Where innocence was at its best
And love would make a comfy nest

I had to learn to fly alone
I had to face the great unknown

And in the process hurt and pain
And when I failed to try again

Or would I stay here as a child
Unsure bewildered all the while

And never reach and never see
That golden place, maturity

MELODY

It's lurking there inside my brain
That haunting lyrical refrain
And seems I cannot bring to fore
And it is one that I adore

I used to hum it all the time
I knew each nuance, knew each line
I used to sing it on my way
I sounded just like Doris Day

But now it's just a memory
Embedded in posterity
I don't believe what I am told
That this will happen when you're old

But wait
A momentary lapse was all
I hear it now yes I recall
The tune and words are flowing back
An orchestra is all I lack
You should be here to hear each note
I think it's something Porter wrote
I love that lilting sweet refrain
I hope I don't forget again

WAITING FOR SUMMER

I can hardly wait for summer
When the snow is off the ground
I miss the green of meadow
When the trees are bare all round
With their gnarled and naked branches
That shows a nest or two
While in summer with the leaves
Are hidden from my view

I can hardly wait for summer
To hear the robins song
When the days just stretch forever
And the evenings linger long
As I labor through the winter
I see no beauty there
Not in the frost upon the pane
The white snow everywhere

Why can't I see the beauty?
In a crisp cold winters day
The ice upon the hanging bough
The snowflakes where they lay
I know that it is resting time
For all that thirst to grow
I know that seeds like buttercups
Just wait beneath the snow

I must learn to love the winter
For I'm missing half my days
While I'm longing for the summer
The years will go their ways
For the seasons mark the passing time
Each one of to share
To savor and to cherish
As long as it is there

OUR FEELLINGS

I love it in the evening when the candles lit
It stirs my heart from where I sit
And seems it's all for me this shadow view

For you it may be seen in early morn
A gray wet garden all forlorn
A baby bird perched on a bough
It's really all the same somehow

THE FAR AWAY

Long ago and far away
A place we know but cannot stay
We search the rubble of our mind
For things we yearn but cannot find
In the hours of today
The things we need but threw away
The soft warm memories that cling
The change each memory will bring
The edges of the far away
Are rounded smooth by passing day
And sail into our vision sweet
A tiny twinge with each heart beat
And as we find them hidden there
We savor each with hidden tear
We take them back or set them free
For what we are in memory
Is but a narrow image now
A guide to show the when the how
The past is there to lean upon
For when our life is nearly gone
The long ago and far away
Now seems to linger and to stay
The sad the bad will melt like ice
The good, we multiply it twice
Delusion cannot cause us harm
To view the past without alarm
And as we head to far away
We live the long ago today

GOOD FRIENDS

To fill my time with friends is my design
For days are precious hours I can't waste
I fill my book of memories each day
With chosen few, and not in haste

For I will seek them out in days ahead
And hold them oh so very close
And nurture and care for
All those I love the most

For this is all I have when
I have walked the last long mile
When friends become companions
To hold my hand and smile

WHAT HAS BECOME OF ME

When did my days of happy end, when years allotted me
Seemed shadows of some other time, to vague to even see

And I a stranger stood to fill, a space I could not find
I even lost the pictured past, it would not come to mind

There was no yesterday for me, all memories were dead
I stored no promises of hope, in what strange voices said

And passing through each night and day, and gentle though they be
I serve no purpose, thus I think, what has become of me

DAYS

Days each lay in wait, to take our time
To spin our years to stories, yours and mine
The plans we have in head and heart, are changed as minutes fly
As if we had no will at all, we watch the time go by

But still we plan the years ahead, as if in this we see
Our dreams emerge, and thus take shape into reality
We must push forth, even if our life is changed complete
We try to learn a lesson with mistakes that we repeat

We try and try for this is life, we live what we believe
We rectify our days and years and thus we may achieve
The warp and weave, the cloth of years
That makes the garment each one wears

WE ARE SHADOWS

We are shadows on the earth
And only to ourselves are real
Our thoughts are silent, dreams unknown
Our words forgotten less we kneel

When we are gone, never missed
Even if we're loved awhile
A fleeting thing this passion
A tiny memory a smile

It's but a ghost in thought
To tantalize, then slip away
There is nothing left of me
That isn't back in yesterday

THE LULLABY

The lullabies have never left her lips
The baby cries still linger in her ear
Upon her face etched in every weary line
Is everyday spent, of every single year

And still she looks upon this man as child
She holds his hand, and strokes his baby head
As years play tricks with all her minutes spent
She says a prayer, and tucks him into bed

But he has long since followed his own way
And she a distant image of the past
In time will float back in his memory
And he will know and need her love at last

THE DREAMER

There is a dreamer who cannot live
In this my world of woe
She walks in wonder all her days
Her minutes all aglow

She speaks to all of nature
She knows of wondrous things
She feels no cold of winter
Her days are always spring

If tears, they're all for happiness
As days before her lie
No tears of sorrow touch her cheek
She does not grieve like I

But still I know her very well
And it will ever be
She keeps my hopes, and spins my dreams
She lives inside of me

QUIET DESPERATION

I entered into life, but did not choose my way
I was bathed and fed, pushed and led
And finally arrived with fear, today
And now alone I flounder and reach out

For arms to hold, and voices sweet
Just memories of a distant past
While searching faces that I meet
How strange are people that I knew

No music in the words they spoke
I live in quiet desperation
It's time that I awake

IF I COULD HAVE THE MEMORIES

If I could have things as they were
Instead of how they are
I'd just have horse and buggy
There wouldn't be a car
I'd have the warm and friendly talks
And long and friendly, quiet meals
After saying grace
Walks on a summer evening
A swing on every tree
If I could have a second chance
To think of days of yore
To go a little slower
To try again once more
I feel in distant dreamy past
Contentment so sublime
I hear a voice say, hold it fast
There isn't' any time

WAR

Who took my day, for I had plans
Who took my life right from my hands

The time is dark, there is no sun
A noise, a bullet from a gun

Now all my future dreams are dead
Somewhere a name you may have read

I left no child to take my name
The years go on and it's the same

A haunting voice for ever more
There was, there is, there will be war

WE ALL HAVE DREAMS

We all have our dreams to a different degree
We all have our visions we cherish and see
We don't think about it all very much
We seem to be living in such a mad rush

Sometimes we take heed when it's quiet and dark
That we must make the grade, we must make our mark
But with all good intentions the very next day
The business of living sweeps all this away

And suddenly time has the upper hand
Can we now change our ways, if we now take a stand
For older and wiser we all have to face
We haven't done much by the end of the race

And hindsight will shame us, in foresight we're blind
We now see success has left us behind
And nothing will come of the dreams that we weave
It's only the doers that finally achieve

THE DREAMLESS

Dead hearts look out at me---through sombre eyes
Lips speak to cover up---with useless lies
And weary bodies move---to tuneless beat
There dragged ahead each day---by weary feet
And this their life---just shadows grey
They've let their dreams---just slip away
There are no sunshine days ahead, no memories
They're trapped in one long dull eternity

WHO AM I

Some ancient wound predicts my future
Some buried hurt designs each day
Some unheard words, some spoke in anger
I didn't hear somebody say

These acts of long ago will shape me
All hidden from my conscious mind
Deep down within my own subconscious
And guiding me as if I'm blind

And we would falter, we would fall
For no one lives a day alone
For man is as his hours shape him
And man is as his years are honed

IN DREAMS

If when I go I leave you with regret
For things you should have said, and hadn't yet
I'll feel your pain and come to you each night
And stay with you and talk till morning light

For as mortals we do not think of death
We do not think of loved ones laid to rest
There's lots of time for kindness, so we say
But suddenly it is the final day

COME BACK AGAIN

Lost love and quiet times alone
Days filled with memories of the past
And minutes like grey shadows lay
Across my heart, where aching lasts

Only clocks sound in my silent world
No other noise invades my listening ear
I'm bound with change of feelings
Tortured with this past I once held dear

How can I bear the pain of empty years
But still I hold the hurting ever close
For if I let it go, I'll be alone
Without the past I love the most

And so I do not see tomorrow clear
But shaded with my memories of pain
A child of sorrow searching here
A wanting to be whole again

It's only feelings that I seek
A sign like sun behind the rain
That I'll invade your dreams at night
In hopes that you'll come back again

And this pain we feel, we feel alone
A remedy to ease sorrow isn't known
We deal with loss down through the years
With sad memories, and tears, and tears

MY STORY

All these minutes fill the day
And finally they slip, away

And all those minutes gone were mine
But all too soon the end of time

Claims me, and I will mourn no more
Those wasted days, the days of yore

The grey tomorrow takes my sight
The grey tomorrow turns to night

And it is cold, and I am old
I walk the last long weary mile
My story told

GIVING

I hid my real self long ago, deep down inside of me
A child of hope, and love, and faith for all eternity

And built a wall around myself to keep me warm and safe
And no one dared to enter in, a dream land laid to waste

A dungeon deep and dark to keep my secret thoughts
A place to keep my injuries, from all my battles fought

But oh I was so lonely; each day was filled with doubt
I kept myself, unto myself, and kept all true love out

It's only when we dare to trust, and open up our heart
That we receive, while giving, that lets the loving start

BAD LUCK

Nature working at her best
For every animal except
Arrogant hard headed man
Does not conform to any plan
And so we go against the grain
We fuss and grumble and complain
When things don't suit the way we feel
We say we've got a rotten deal
And when we find we're lacking pluck
We blame it all, on our bad luck
We rush ahead till it's too late
But never stop to meditate
Years of thoughtful living gain
Protection from life's daily bane
The only good that we can do
Is leave this earth as much like new
If we are capable of feeling
Let Mother Nature do the healing

Hilda Nightingale

GLAD

As now I live, I wake so brave
I do not think about the grave
I do not look in mirrors, and
I do not worry what's at hand

I face each day, like what I see
I hardly even notice me
And as I face each day I feign
I do not see I've aged or gained

And this is good to some extent
I do not see where vigour went
And I stay young in hope and mind
I leave despair and age behind

And if I go to sleep some night
And feel I have done something right
And do not wake to greet the dawn
I'll still be glad that I was born

XMAS DAY

Snowflakes falling, see them falling
It is nearly Christmastime
Cutting trees to stand for Christmas
Spruce, and fir, and sturdy pine
In the old days there were sleigh rides
And real candles on the tree
Homemade stockings made for children
And red mittens made for me
Christmas songs sung at twilight
Bundled up against the cold
Many voices all together
Christmas carols as of old
Turkeys cooking and plum puddings
Set upon the cupboard side
On the mantel there were stockings
Of all shapes, and stretching wide
Rosie children, just like angels

Oh how good they try to be
When it's Christmas, and they know
Santa's watching, and can see
Every misdeed, so they're cautious
And try to do they're best
Keeping clean, and keeping quiet
Dressed up in their Sunday best
Then the magic moments here
Amid paper on the floor
Forgotten is the Christmas tree
And the wreath upon the door
Santa's been here and we thank him
For the gifts that we received
And everyone is happy
And the parents are relieved
For it's over, yes it's over
And the toys are piled in hills
And we give Mom a great big kiss
And Father gets the bills

WAITING

Dear Lord I wait for you, in clouds
That race across the sky
I wait for you in blowing winds
That scream and moan and sigh

I hear your voice in every tide
That tumbles on the shore
And hear you in each roaring wave
That reach, then are no more

I hear you in the robin's song
And in the crying gull
I hear you in the winter's gale
And in the summers lull

And I have but to give my heart
And nest it in your care
And know that it is home at last
And you'll be waiting here

JUST A LITTLE

Let me be a little light
For all the sad to see
Just a tiny candle
To draw the hurt to me

That I might shed a little glow
To brighten up the day
To help the weary with their load
And speed them on their way

In helping others we can gain
A solace for our woe
For feeling pain of someone else
Is one way that we know

That we are not alone at all
Our paths will intertwine
I walk a stranger's road each day
And they in turn walk mine

And everyday is learning
If we take heed and see
The man that walks beside us all
Reflects what life will be

THE GIFT

One more sunset, seen through my eyes
The reds and yellow gold
That fills the heart, I realize
I treasure till I'm old

No other thing in life so free
That asks for nothing in return
Except your longing just to see
This yellow red and golden burn

That warms the western twilight sky
Then slips away to sleep
But leaves a restful mantle
Velvet deep

Hilda Nightingale

THE LACE OF LIFE

Honest has no place in life
It is too blunt, it is too cold
And shunned by those who dream
Of jaded rest, within it's fold

I see the edge of honesty
The frill and lace of life
The cutting and unkind remarks
Made with a velvet knife

The flowers mean no harm
The clouds are soft and still
The sweet sweet scent of forest breeze
Nature does no man ill will

I choose the warmth of thought
Because I'm me
And live my life serene
And let the others be

NATIVE SONS

Along the mighty Fraser
The red man told his tale
Of the fierce and mighty grizzly
The eagle and the whale
As they had lived forever
Neath the snow-capped mountain dome
Beneath the tall dark Douglas fir
They called B.C. their home
Then came along the trappers
And the seekers out of gold
And the listened to the stories
That the red man gladly told
And from the line of Forty Nine
To B.C.'s frozen north
The white men came to gather
And change all as he went forth
They cleared the mighty forest
The trees mile after mile
The loss of habitation of
The creatures of the wild

They built along the Fraser
Along the rocky shore
The white man stopped the potlatch
And the totem is no more
The red man then was full of fear
And the spirits didn't say
For all the help the red man gave
White men would rule one day
The spirit drum was silent
No hope to fill the hearts
Where as the white man took the land
The Indian departs
But is the story ended
For the nature of the land
Sustains itself, and sees the right
Of every native band
For the spirits live in every tree
And stone upon the shore
The eagle is a brother
The bear is in their lore
We know the wolf, the beaver,
And the deer cohabitate
Could all men learn to do the same
Or must we wait

LIKE THEM

Was that a bird that spoke to me
Once on a summers day
A flower singing joyously
As I walked along the way
And as I passed a giant oak
A leaf dropped in my hand
Then as I sat besides the pond
I heard the bullfrog band
When I lounged in golden grass
A snake lay by my side
He caught the insects as they passed
I watched them as they died
I felt no fear but sadness
For life as it must be
As nature's plan is acted on
For nothing's really free
And I like any other thing
Will have my summer's day
Will live my autumn, winter spring
Then pass along the way

THAT'S A LAUGH

Thinking of thirty, could make me feel old
And I tried to erase from my mind
That my now, thick black hair, will not be here
And my face could be wrinkled and lined

Thinking of fifty, a vague future day
That comes to us, all except me
I push it behind, not feeling too kind
To these ancient pictures I see

Thinking of eighty, now I would be wise
And sorting the slag from the gold
And laugh at my youth, now knowing the truth
That thirty could make me feel old

REACHING

I found a lovely place to stay
With blues so blue, and greens so green
It took my breath away
And daisies like white linen
Where all their beauty lie, a star black night
So close, that one may reach
Their arms into the sky
And everything is sensuous
And all one heart can bear
And this in just a moment
Standing there

Hilda Nightingale

WHEN I GROW UP

When I grow, and I am tall
I will not listen, not at all
To folks that give their good advice
And tell me once, and tell me twice
To pick up all my clothes and toys
And don't play rough, that's just for boys
And listen when I'm spoken to
But never thank me when I do
I will not eat a single green
Or tell a soul where I have been
Or wear my rubbers in the rain
Or do my homework once again
Or go to bed when I am told
Or pay attention when they scold
I'll eat candy, I'll eat cake
And I'll sit up and keep awake
I'll only do the things I like
I'll go for miles upon my bike
And I'll stay up and watch T.V.
And tell them all, to let me be
When I grow up and I am tall
There will just be me----oh yes, my doll

Father smiled and did not scoff
And mother said, "She's dozing off."

THE GHOST

The house was dark and empty
Folks say it's haunted, but me
I know, the people that's passed and gone
Come back for a cup of tea

The walls that rang with laughter
The firelights empty glow
And the rocking chair
That's vacant now, is rocking to and fro

As I look through the window, I see them
Afraid of this silent place
Of the spirit of people that's passed away
That live in a state of grace

And it saddens my spirit intensely
If only they could know
I'd like to be friends, in the present
As I will be as soon as they go

I WILL NOT LIVE IN VAIN

It matters not, that I someday
Will lay immobile with decay
And never more to grace the eye
For where I've gone they call it die
It matters more each day I find
That I may never cross the mind
Of all the loved one's left behind
There must be something left of me
To pass on to humanity
To last until eternity
It may be just a verse or song
Some goodness that I pass along
And pray it not be something wrong
I will not mind the quiet and the dark
Though death has stilled the spark
Now, but rest, waiting, quiet, content
And know I have not lived in vain
Till someone to my grave is sent
To take me home again

A CALL HOME

Did God send you back to me
But in another guise
I seem to know your every move
I seem to know your eyes

The pain is dulled and faded
When I hold you to my breast
As if I had no loss at all
The agony is less

For God is good, and knows my pain
And though it takes awhile
He fills me up with hope again
Because I am his child

We take His love and walk our path
But never are alone
He holds our hand, and guides our steps
Until He calls us home

SOUL OF WONDER

I'm the type to fill my soul with wonder
I pause to see the sunrise in the morn
I hear music in the distant thunder
And I thank God each day that I was born

I walk by hour in forest's cool green splendour
I hear the wind, my heart swells in my breast
I say a prayer for all that is created
When I see the tiny egg within the nest

So I'm glad I searched so long and deep
I'm glad that I took such care
To live in such a wonder land
And just see beauty there

MY TREE

I can no longer see the branches
From my window at the side
Of the giant tree, where as a child
I used to play and hide

The wind was rough, and had its way
With both the limb and bough
The lacy fronds are broken, gone
This saddens me somehow

It's like a friend that is no more
That waited just outside my door
I feel an emptiness inside
A place I used to play and hide

That lovely friend, my willow tree
Still grows on in memory

EACH DAY

Each day deceives me with a dream
That stirs my heart
And makes new promises and says
A brand new start
And I forget the dreams before
And how they wane
With unkept vows and faded hopes
I dream again
Because one day I'll greet the dawn
And then arise
And all the minutes will be pure
Till sunlight dies
And waiting will be worth
The effort made
And I will rest content
My wanting laid
For some a dream is seen
Through times of pain
The dreamless search each day
And search in vain

But life is made of days all fresh and new
And what you use them for is up to you

WELL WORN PATHS

As I walked the road of life
There's paths to left and paths to right
I often wondered had I turned
What things in life I could have learned

The changes that I could have made
The different choices never weighed
I did not change because of fear
And thoughts that it may cost too dear

I took the easy gentle route
I did not turn and look about
I just faced front, and straight ahead
And put my feet where others led

And as I look back on my days
I see them only in a haze
No deeds stand out to make me proud
Though second chances were allowed

I followed paths all ready made
And lived with plans all ready laid

REGRETS

If I could reach inside myself
And grasp the hurt, and tear it out
If I could change my jumbled thoughts
To see at last what it's about

If I could stop these flowing tears
Or soothe this weary aching heart
Oh I would change, I tell myself
If I could have another start

But we must live with our regrets
Our misspent days are with us all
And in the quiet and the dark
We see them beckon, hear them call

Sometimes so faint we hardly see
But still they will not let us be
They are the price that we must pay
For everything we do and say

GOD TAKES MY HAND

Behind my heart where all my broken dreams are kept
And all the words I cannot say
And all the tears I have not wept
God sees it all and knows me deep
He stirs my weary aching heart
And wakens all the dreams that sleep
And takes my hand, and leads me on
To my tomorrow

FEELING BLESSED

I hold you oh so close you see
Because you are a part of me

Tomorrow is so far away
And sadness is another day

Now is only warmth, and well
The feelings that no words can tell

And I will forfeit all the rest
To hold this gift, of feeling blessed

THE LITTLE TREE

I saw a little tree alone
In hard packed earth, beside a stone
It's growing shaded from the sun
And seeded where no waters run
Frustrated at its every try
I wondered if it would not die
And as I passed it everyday
Sometimes it stood, sometimes it lay
And I was filled with empathy
Each time I passed this little tree
Sometimes with all my worldly care
I did not see it standing there
Then how surprising it would be
When once again, I saw this tree
For it had grown, and now stood tall
I could not see the stone at all
And I hugged close the pride I felt
As if some way my interest helped
And with it all I learned that I
Must face all odds, and try, and try
For this is where our growing lies
From seedlings, till the day we die

A REMEMBERED LOVE

They say first loves don't last
All new with eagerness to start
Then kept alive in memory
And tucked within the heart

To be released some future day
Relive this love, this hope and pain
To be returned to memories file
And tucked into the heart again

LOVE IS LIKE THAT

It asks no questions, no reward
It's constant, selfless, kind
Committed to just one, that's love
And never out of mind

It rests secure within the heart
In every dream it lives
Its needs are great, and feeds upon
The lovers need to give

It grows without the taking
It's in itself unique
It stands alone, the one thing
That all the world would seek

The cause of pain and heartaches
The cause of joy supreme
Though love is but a feeling
And love cannot be seen

A priceless gift, we cannot lose
When it's returned by those we choose

THANK YOU GOD

Restful moments close my days
And fill my thoughts with thankful praise
For all the things God does for me, in many ways
And I am full of sorrow for the words I cannot find

To thank Him for His blessings, in my heart and mind
I think He sees my lack of prose
The love for Him that fills my heart
I think He knows

WILL I LOVE AGAIN

No more tears will dim my eyes, or wet my cheek
No more loves will hurt my heart, or make my limbs go weak
No more arms will hold me close, or hands caress
No more sleepless nights, except from loneliness

For I have deeply loved and lost
And in the quiet hours counted cost
For all I gave, my payment has been pain
So, if I meet a new love, will I love again?

MORNING MIST ON MY GARDEN

Dismembered fragments, not seen clear
Surprise is given vent
I cannot see the violets
I wonder where they went

Behind a dream like haze
Half here, half there
Just promises in future
Even as I stare

A rootless rose floats by
Hidden by chiffon
A changing scene of bush and tree
By magic, on and on

And I am in an unknown world
But as the sun ascends
It plants this floating spectacle
And I am home again

I WAS MEANT TO

I was meant to take tea in my garden
With a friend or two or three
I was meant to sit and dream awhile
And fall in love with the sea

I was meant to greet the morning
With a dawn all silver and grey
And the promise of a golden song
Of the tall trees whispered sway

I was meant to feel in the evening
A prayer of thanks on high
For another day, with the love of God
And contentment where I lie

THE GIVERS

The world is full of takers, that only givers know
They wait upon the takers, without the pomp and show
Just quietly partaking in every given task
Performing every duty that the takers seem to ask
And years go by so swiftly, and suddenly we find
The givers learn and prosper, and leave the takers far behind

For in giving, so we gather in abundance everywhere
We're sought out and remembered, even takers hold us dear
For the givers are not thinking, the thought is not in mind
For all we do for others, we are repaid in kind
In living as a giver, and putting others first
Life looks unto the future, and we are reimbursed
We pass each day as it's sent, and do not look that far
We live our life as givers, because that's what we are

MY SHADOW

I can see my shadow
High up on the wall
It's awful tall and skinny
It's not like me at all

When I move it wiggles
It dances to and fro
I cannot lose it if I try
It follows where I go

But when the day is dull and grey
And the sun just doesn't shine
I cannot see my shadow
It's awful hard to find

Sometimes I miss my shadow
But on a sunny day
I see my shadow once again
It's back again to play

TIME USERS

Had I used my minutes wisely
All my hours would be gold
And the years would flow by gently
With no regrets, now I am old

But I like all the fools abroad
Threw time to left and right
And finally saw the years of waste
But only in hindsight

A VISIT TO GRAMMA

"Can I come in?" Said a voice from the door
With his face all full of jam
"I want to come and talk awhile
I'm a friend of yours I am"
I invited him in and he sat on a chair
And we talked of the weather, foul and fair
And people and things of other nations
And various other conversations
And then we had cookies, and there were we
Dunking them in our cup of tea
And he left his teddy, just for a lend
Only because he was my friend
And when he left, I had to say
What a wonderful way to start my day

LIFE'S MUSIC

I thought I was alone just now
But then I heard the brook
And little fish were swimming there
And so I took a look
I saw a frog just sleeping
A cricket happened by
I heard the stirrings of the air
With sparrows flying high
I noticed blue flags nodding
They brushed a blade of grass
And made a note of music
Each time I saw them pass
And as I sat so quiet
I realized that I
Was party to a symphony
So sweet it made me cry
I became a part of life
And it a part of me
I understood the flora
I knew the mighty tree
It was all so beautiful
I could not stir at all
I lingered with the dying day
I heard the evening call
I waited till the velvet sky
Was studded diamond bright
And watched the wonders of the day
Turn to the black of night
And, for just a little while
I felt I was a part
Of all of God's creations, and
This wonder filled my heart

FAITH

Betrayed by hope, that always springs eternal
In the heart of those who reach for the stars
And learn no lesson in their failure
Using the dawn to launch new dreams

Wearing their days proudly
Hiding their disappointment in the night
Turning their faces to the sky, with anticipation and a smile

And moving forward

SOMEDAY

Someday my mind will lollygag
And I will sleep at night
For all things will be shiny clean
And everything done right

But now I have to think about
And sometimes make a list
To keep in mind odd things to do
And things that I have missed

My life could well be tranquil
If ever comes the day
My mind can guiltless, lollygag
And throw the list away

WHAT WOULD YOU DO

What will I do with today I thought
It's bright and shiny new
If you had a day just like this
Tell me, what would you do
Would you just sit here and think awhile
Would you go for a nice long walk
And would you take a friend along
To play or have a talk
Would you speak to the flowers along the way
Would you listen to the brook
Or lie on your back and watch the clouds
No matter how long it took
Would you visit someone who is lonely
Would you share a feeling or two
For when you share, it shows you care
Tell me what would you do
Sometimes, when a day is so beautiful
It slips very quickly by
And we don't hear the song of the bluebird
Or see a butterfly
If you pause to be thankful for such a day
And be thankful that you are you
And if we meet on such a day
Would you tell me, what you would do

HEAVEN'S GATES

If I was guarding heaven's gates
And saw who entered there
I'd make room for only those
Who always did their share

I'd stop the shirkers on the spot
And send them back again
To do what they had left undone
Though it may be in vain

I'd let the little children in
And those who knew the Lord
And all those with a pure heart
Where only love was stored

And then I'd search my own heart
And if one sin I see
I'd have to shut tight heaven's gates
There'd be no room for me

IF THEY GO AWAY

I see her at the window
With the sunlight in her hair
I see her watch the laneway
When twilight's creeping near

And she hardly seems to tire
With her vigil everyday
As she watches for her loved ones
Since first they went away

And if longing brings them ever close
They should be here right now
For the yearnings always with her
As the lines across her brow

But hope will spring eternal
In the hearts of those who care
And lives within her mind each day
As if they're always here

SUNLIGHT

Sunlight, sneaking through cracks in fences
Under partly drawn shades
Uninvited, unashamed, allowing no privacy
Through tree limbs, bold, unchecked
Afraid of no one, except the night
Bribing the moon to tell when she sleeps
So he can
Sneak through cracks in fences
Under partly drawn shades

A SECOND CHANCE

When I was small I thought of things
Of castles, clouds, and mighty kings
I knew that they were dreams, of course
When I saw visions of a horse
That danced a waltz with flowing mane
With just the south winds soft refrain
And frogs upon a lily pad
That croaked a chorus, bright or sad
And tall grass bending to and fro
To natures tunes I didn't know

But now I'm old, I look and see
The smaller version that was me
Back in the past that was so soft
The picture clouds that float aloft
The years, the waste, the in between
The time I didn't even dream
I feel the tears, the ache within
For all the dreams that might have been
But shook off age, and searched the sky
I did not ask life, what or why
But heard again youths sweet refrain
And listened, as I dream again

A SMALL HOPE

All these days I gathered
Have flown away in years
All the sad songs I have sung
Have run away in tears

And I am spent and empty
A dreamless soul, a shell
With no more love to give
And no more words to tell

And so I gather dead dreams
Not let them slip away
To breathe into these dead dreams, life
To bring back yesterday

MISERY

Oh how I loved my misery
I cherished it each day
And held it ever close to me
Not letting it away
It filled my heart it filled my mind
It hid away the sun
And made each day, all dark with gloom
Each and every one
But it was mine, and mine alone
And something I don't share
It came from pain and loneliness
When no one seemed to care
When it was gone it left with me
A vacant hollow heart
Void of feeling, waiting there
For misery to start

HEREDITARY

From the family I have grown
A flower of my heritage I be
Part of one and some other, propagate
I will be like no other you will see

And yet there will be pictures of the past
In things I do, and in my works each day
To haunt your mind and tease your memory
In everything I do and things I say

I cannot separate myself from bygone years
They color me and mine until I die
But leave behind a tiny glimpse of me
That they will live, and pass along like I

The years may fade the flowers of the past
But leave their perfume in those left to grow
Down through the spring and fall of years
A hybrid strain, a haunting yet to know

DAYS NO MORE

Oh these days that are no more
Slipped through fingers of thought
Lay in wasteland there unused
Now in memory are caught

And I grieve in retrospect
Though I know it is in vain
For lost time cannot be saved
Or wasted minutes used again

THE KING

Sol said, "I'll chase the morning mist
Across the valley floor
I'll give each tree a golden glow
Each blade of grass and more

I'll sparkle on each grain of sand
That's washed by every wave
And warm the hearts of mighty kings
And every lowly knave

For I am life and start each day
I reign in kingdoms hall
Around the world, I never sleep
For I am mighty Sol."

THE GOLDEN DOOR

Go and fetch her, bring her to me
She has wearied oh so long
In life's battles she had courage
In her living she was strong

Did God's bidding helping others
As she struggled with each day
Only asking help from Jesus
As she bent her head to pray

And she never asked of Jesus
Anything just for herself
Just for others did she seek Him
Just for others pray for help

And the angels took her gently
Brought her through that golden door
Up to sit in Jesus' glory
Where life's worries are no more

THE CLEANSING

I envy you your tears
For you will laugh tomorrow
While I dry eyed will grieve
For all my woes and sorrow

To take life lightly
May be fine for some
Their grief short lived
They take each day as it may come

But I hold close to me each bitter word
And live each hurt until the end
I feel the friction that they cause
And grow to know them as a friend

Tomorrow I'll look back and see
The sad lost days that needn't be
The wasted time, the stolen years
I envy you your tears

THE END

Printed in the United States
139722LV00002B/5/P

9 781434 379962